T0282104

Praise for Christopher Brookhouse

"Th[is] character-driven narrative focuses not so much on generating excitement as on painting compelling portraits. [In *A Mind of Winter,*] Brookhouse writes with a gentle charm, expressed through edgy, efficient dialogue and tightly constructed prose that uses single moments to create vivid snapshots that propel the story forward at a languid but deliberate pace..."

— Kirkus Reviews —

[*Messing with Men*] ... follows aging residents in a resort town as they fall in and out of love and lust with each other, dabble in local causes, and try to make sense of their lives...These wryly reflective Floridian retirees, with their longings and regrets, will remain with readers.

—Booklife—

"Brookhouse's writing is so good and so elegant ... [*Percy's Field*] is not a fast-paced thriller that emphasizes action. Rather, this novel moves slowly in the Carolina humidity, and the emphasis is placed on the immaculate prose and the deep characterization given to Harr County and North Carolina's tobacco country. ... The book excels at presenting a dark and enjoyable murder story that resonates with the truth that the past is never really over."

— from a *Foreword* Clarion Review —

"*FINN* is the real thing—a southern Gothic tale in which the narrator must solve the mystery of his own nature in order to escape the web of violence in which he is caught. Start it when you have time to finish because you won't want to put it down."

— Terry Roberts, author of
A Short Time to Stay Here and winner of the
Willie Morris Award for Southern Fiction

"[*FINN* is a] novel to be savored more than once. Written with the same languorous, rumbling passion of Paul Newman and Joanne Woodward's film *The Long Hot Summer.*"

— Kirkus Reviews —

"[*Silence* is a] memorable story by a talented writer who understands women better than most women understand themselves."

— Doris Betts —

"[*Silence*] is a quiet novel of personal and seasonal challenges set in a small town in New Hampshire. Brookhouse writes confidently and unobtrusively about authentic issues."

— Kirkus Reviews —

"Christopher Brookhouse has produced another literary wonder in *Old-Timer*. It is both easy to read and playfully complex."

— Rob Neufeld —
Asheville Citizen-Times

"[*Old-Timer* is one] of the best novel releases by one of the best authors you haven't heard about."

— Tom Mayer —
New Bern Sun Journal

Other Titles
by Christopher Brookhouse

FICTION

Running Out

Wintermute

Passing Game

Fog: The Jeffrey Stories

Old-Timer

A Selfish Woman

Silence

Loving Ryan

Finn

9 Pruitt

Messing with Men

The Gus Salt Series

A Pinch of Salt

Percy's Field

Nolan's Cross

A Mind of Winter

POETRY

Scattered Light

The Light Between the Fields

How It Was

CHRISTOPHER BROOKHOUSE

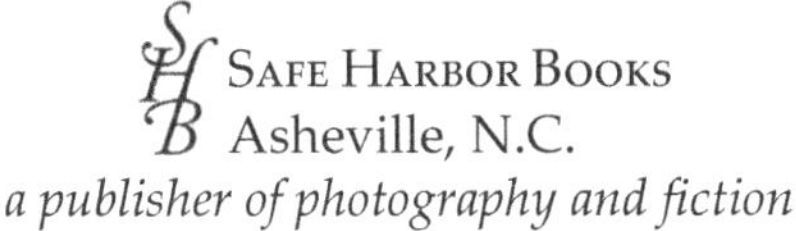

SHB
Safe Harbor Books
Asheville, N.C.
a publisher of photography and fiction

Safe Harbor Books
1 Page Avenue, #404
Asheville, NC 28801
www.safeharborbooks.com

First Edition

 This is a work of fiction. Characters, incidents, and dialogue derive from the author's imagination and any resemblance to people, living or dead, or to events, past or present, is purely coincidental.

ISBN: 978-1-7344995-2-0 (trade paperback)

Library of Congress Cataloging-in-Publication Data

Names: Brookhouse, Christopher, 1938- author.
Title: How it was / Christopher Brookhouse.
Description: First edition. | Asheville, N.C. : Safe Harbor Books, 2023. | Summary: "The year is 1980. Leonard Grey, now in his sixth year at a prestigious Southern college, works various jobs to pay for the remaining class hours he needs to graduate. Hired by the athletic department to tutor a superb Black basketball recruit, Lenny becomes ensnared in conflicting conspiracies-one to use the player's skills for personal and institutional enrichment, the other to preserve the school's predominantly white athletic teams and tradition of academic excellence. Discredited by the college, Lenny is hired as a full-time security guard, which entangles him in the details of a local girl's mysterious disappearance and the murkiness of local politics. This time, however, the young man has a chance to heal the wounds of his own past."-- Provided by publisher.
Identifiers: LCCN 2023024853 (print) | LCCN 2023024854 (ebook) | ISBN 9781734499520 (trade paperback) | ISBN 9781734499537 (epub)
Subjects: LCGFT: Novels.
Classification: LCC PS3552.R658 H69 2023 (print) | LCC PS3552.R658 (ebook) | DDC 813/.54--dc23/eng/20230602
LC record available at https://lccn.loc.gov/2023024853
LC ebook record available at https://lccn.loc.gov/2023024854

Cover photograph adapted from "Abandoned Barn, Mebane, North Carolina 2006" by Bill Bamberger, billbamberger.com

Printed in the USA.

For Junius and Leonard

Chapel Hill days are not forgotten.

How It Was

Part I
Going Dark

I

He knew her name was Maisie. He had waited on her before, December a year ago. She ordered a daiquiri and refused to show him her ID, but he served her anyway, and her father, Professor Thorne, left him a substantial tip. Maisie looked like most of the college girls then—long hair, mini skirt, boots. She eyed him with contempt. Her boots, as the song said, were made for walking—walking all over him. Now, in the summer night, she tried to focus on his face and didn't manage that too well. This time no boots. No clothes at all.

Leonard Grey. Lenny. Residence: Prester, North Carolina. Occupation: student when he can afford it. Otherwise, waiter. Otherwise, handy with tools and knows a bit about cars. Prester College is six miles, mostly uphill on Forest Road, from his '50s Airstream rusting on a patch of grass surrounded by second-growth forest and kudzu. The Bower, a development of houses built around a lake, is a half mile in the opposite direction. The Bower is private. Residents only.

The Buick Skylark was angled into the weeds. Maisie sprawled on the seat, her head near the passenger's door. A striped beach towel spread across the gritty floor mat. Lenny guessed she'd had a lot to drink. Her silver anklet shone in the light of the quarter moon, but most of her lay in shadows.

He opened the door, knelt in the weeds, and brushed her hair away from her eyes. "Don' touch," she said.

"You can't stay here."

She groped for the towel. "Who you?" He wanted to laugh at the way she said it, but he didn't.

"Lenny."

"Lake. Forgot."

"Forgot what?"

"Clothes."

Keys dangled from the ignition. He tucked her arm against her side and eased the door shut. He opened the driver's door, lifted her legs, and squeezed under them. "I'll get you home," he said.

He drove past the trailer where he lived and continued uphill toward the village and the college. Summer school was over. The village was silent, the campus deserted. When he ran track, the team used to do morning runs through the neighborhood where the Thornes lived. A security light flooded a pale glow across the pavers. A sweep of yard, trees, bushes, and gauzy shadows. The house was Midcentury Modern, lots of stucco and glass.

Lenny helped Maisie out of the car and draped the blanket over her shoulders. She leaned on him, her skin cool and moist. The house was unlocked. He promised to return the car in the morning. He wasn't sure she heard him.

The Skylark was ten years old and much faster than his twenty-year-old Jeep. Smelled better too. The sticker on the windshield said Bower Resident. One night a girl who lived there had invited him to swim...and other things. He had a good idea where he would find Maisie's clothes. He stopped at the trailer for a flashlight. His trash can was toppled again. People said they had seen a bear. So had he, but spelled differently.

The first owners had built homes along the shore. There was a swimming beach created for later residents whose hillside homes overlooked the lake. One o'clock. Lights on in a couple of houses, the moon a blur upon the water. Lenny parked in the empty area above the beach and walked down to the shore. Crickets choired in the grass. He remembered the time before. The girl led him to a copse of willows. They talked and kissed and forgot about swimming. She took off her top. Her breasts reminded him of a Bouguereau nude, too perfect to touch. She'd take everything off if he would. He wouldn't. You're no fun, she said.

Past the willows Lenny saw an empty vodka bottle and clothes strewn across the ground. He folded them and tucked them under his arm. A light flared in his face. A voice told him to hold it.

The man coughed and switched off the light. Lenny blinked until he could see again. The man wore a white shirt with short sleeves. A belt with a holstered pistol held up baggy jodhpurs tucked into black boots.

"Earlier tonight I saw the Thorne girl smooching with the DeFoe kid. Her car's here, but she isn't."

"I took her home."

"And you are?"

"Leonard."

"Last name?"

"Grey."

"I'm Warner." He pointed to Security stitched above his shirt pocket. "Whose clothes you got?"

"Hers, I think."

"Skinny dipping and other naked activities are against the rules, but I let it go. Mr. DeFoe is president of the Residents' Association and my boss." Warner pointed to a house across the lake. "He doesn't like me reporting his son's behavior. Boys will be boys and all that."

Warner picked up the vodka bottle and looked Lenny over. "Dressed like you are, I suppose you were jogging or planning to."

"I was just heading out when I saw Miss Thorne's car on the side of the road."

"Heading out from where?"

"The trailer on the way to town."

"Should have figured. You rent from Dodson. That's his house across from us on the shore. Be warned. Bears are back. They may be strays or just passing through, but they're dangerous, especially if cubs are with them. Don't think they're cute and get close."

"I'm careful," Lenny said.

They walked up hill to the parking area. "The person whose clothes you're carrying, be careful of her too. A Thorne can get under your skin."

Warner's pickup was parked next to the Skylark. Lenny told him he waited tables at the Nook. Business was slow until the college started again. He needed more work, but no one was hiring. "Keep you in mind," Warner said. "I know where you live."

❧

Ten o'clock. A bright morning. Hint of autumn in the air. By noon the humidity would take over. Dog days again. After all, it was August.

Mrs. Thorne opened the front door and glanced past Lenny at the Skylark. "You borrow it or steal it?"

"Last night Maisie needed a driver."

"This morning she needed aspirin and coffee." Blonde, tan, and slender, Mrs. Thorne leaned in the doorway. Lenny could see a brown bikini under her white robe. "I'm grateful you assisted her, but I'm not interested in details. I'm annoyed she's here at all. I expected to have the house to myself."

"What went wrong?"

"I've lost count." Mrs. Thorne shaded her eyes from the sun. "I suppose you require a ride to wherever you came from."

Lenny waited by the car. Mrs. Thorne reappeared wearing a T-shirt, jeans, and tennis shoes. He remarked that the driveway needed power washing. "That's Thomas's department," she said. "He's my husband."

Lenny drove. She studied his face. "The Nook. You work there."

"Sometimes."

"Sometimes anything else?"

"Finishing my course work."

"From the looks of you, you've been at it awhile."

"Six years."

"Where are you from?"

"Maine."

"Never been past New Jersey."

She rummaged through the glove compartment for a cigarette. “I keep trying to quit.” The cigarette she found was too stale to smoke. “How did you end up here?”

“I had two scholarship offers—Prester and Dartmouth. I’m not fond of cold winters.”

“So you were poor and smart?”

“Poor and fast. Track scholarship.”

“The team used to run by the house.”

“I was one of those.”

“Six years later you’re still here. What happened?”

“I quit the team. No more scholarship. I pay my way.”

Mrs. Thorne leaned back and closed her eyes. “Don’t we all.”

Lenny turned onto Forest Road. Summer had been dry. The walnut trees were already losing their leaves. “We’re here,” he said.

She opened her eyes and beheld the trailer. “You live in that?”

“You must have seen it before.” Lenny pointed to the Bower sticker. “On your way to the lake.”

“Maisie wangled it. She stuck it on the Skylark because her car is too small for the activities she’s fond of, so she uses mine. Anyway, hers doesn’t run.” Mrs. Thorne got out and kicked one of the soup cans scattered in the grass. “You should eat better.”

She leaned against the Skylark and took off her Ray-Bans. “And I should be sweeter. I appreciate you bringing her home and not taking advantage. You didn’t, did you?”

The question annoyed him. “No, ma’am,” he said.

“You mentioned the driveway.” Lenny told her he charged four dollars an hour. “The kitchen faucet drips. Know how to fix it?" He did. "What about cars?" The basics. "Four an hour seems high." He said he was worth it.

She nodded. "Put what you need on my account at Buck's." She settled into the driver's seat of the Skylark. "I'm not always so bitchy," she said.

❧

LENNY RENTED A POWER WASHER at Buck's Hardware on College Street. Mrs. Thorne was right—he agreed he should eat better. He walked down the block to the drugstore. A smiling Miss Vickie took his order—tuna salad sandwich and a fountain Coke. From his seat at the counter, he watched a family photographing each other at the entrance to the campus, where the bronze figure of Caedmon Prester, for whom the village and the college are named, stands perpetual guard.

"Where you been keeping?" Vickie asked.

"A trailer on Forest Road."

"Lonely out there. You got company? A girl or a dog or something?"

"When I asked for your company, you turned me down."

"Where would a Black gal like me go with a white boy like you? Both of us would be in trouble."

"I'm always hopeful."

"About what?"

"You'll change your mind."

"Don't trust what's on yours. You still in school?"

"When I can afford it."

"You should have kept that scholarship."

"I like running by myself, not with a pack of other people."

"At least you have a choice. Some of us don't."

Lenny finished his sandwich. Vickie totaled his check. He left a dollar tip. She pushed it back. "Liked seeing you again."

"Does that mean I should keep asking for your company?"

"Might." She winked. "Might not too."

Lenny's Jeep didn't like hot and humid. Finally, it started. He parked in the shade of a mimosa by the Thornes' garage. The door was up. He admired the Jaguar, bright and polished. Dust covered the Bug next to it. The Skylark wasn't to be seen.

He located a spigot and hooked up the power washer. Two hours later Mrs. Thorne came out of the house and complimented him on his work. She wore a long thin shirt—or a short sheer dress. He could see her bathing suit under it.

"Are you staring because you like what you see or because you think I'm too old for a bikini?"

"You reminded me of something."

"That's vague. Something what?"

"Summers in Maine. Girls lying on a rocky beach." He remembered the way they tucked and folded their modest bathing suits to show more skin.

"Any girl in particular?"

"One."

"First love?"

"Sort of."

"I suppose vagueness becomes you. Let's go inside and inspect my plumbing problem."

Living room: Cool air, lots of natural light, blond furniture. Kitchen: Dark cabinets, white appliances. He had never seen granite countertops before. The faucet dripped. "Needs a new washer," Lenny said.

"Don't have one on you, do you?"

"Fix it tomorrow."

"You're sweaty. A swim?"

Out the window Lenny saw chaises, chairs, and a round table shaded by a striped umbrella. A cabana was on the other side of the pool. "No suit," he said.

"My house, my rules. None required."

"Mrs. Thorne—"

"*Lia.*" She smiled. "I've embarrassed you. I apologize. At least stick around for a glass of wine. Thomas considers himself an oenophile. I think that's the word. He has some excellent vintages. I remember the time you waited on us. He was impressed with the bottle you recommended."

"I thought about sommelier school."

"Maybe you missed your calling."

They sat by the pool. Lia poured a riesling, much drier than Lenny expected. They touched glasses. "Dog days, I love them," she said. "Heat, humidity, and solitude—except this year dear Maisie has returned."

He asked from where. "Colorado. She failed her summer school courses. The dean requested she absent herself—permanently. Thomas called in some favors. Prester agreed to let her enroll fall semester. As a favor to me, she is looking for digs elsewhere."

"I noticed the Jaguar."

"Thomas's. Mine in the summer while he's away exploring."

"Exploring what?"

"The Civil War is his specialty and battlefields his hobby. This year some remote site in Tennessee."

"He's a popular teacher," Lenny said.

"So I've heard." Lia sipped her wine and watched a hawk glide down the sky.

"Tell me about the Bower."

"Pricey. Few faculty can afford to live there. The residents feel entitled. The children are no exception. Lots of bad behavior. Tanner, Maisie's friend, is better than some others. His father is a top-gun investor. DeFoe Capital. It was his idea to dam some streams, create a lake, sell lots, and get rich, which he and his partners were already."

"I met Warner."

"He's been around forever. When the college had football, he was an assistant coach. You live up the road. If he likes you, he wouldn't stop you from sneaking in for a swim."

"The road around the lake would be a good place to run."

"Mr. Tittle might shoot you."

"Who is he?"

"A man with a temper. He's shot at bikers before. The police warned him, but Bower people live by their own rules. It's always open season on trespassers."

Lenny finished his wine and promised to return in the morning to fix the faucet and look over Maisie's Bug.

❧

WARNER HAD TAPED A NOTE to the trailer door: "Might have some work." There was a phone number, but Lenny didn't have a phone. Tomorrow he'd ask Lia to use hers.

In the morning the Jeep's brake pedal sank to the floor. Toolbox in one hand, Lenny stuck out the other, cocked his thumb, and started walking. Two cars passed him. A patrol car went by in the opposite direction, turned around, and stopped ahead of him. Dressed in a beige uniform, the officer leaned on the car, arms crossed.

"Something wrong?" Lenny asked.

The officer took off his sunglasses and pushed them into his shirt pocket. "Where you coming from?" Lenny pointed to the trailer. "You're in the village limits. There's an ordinance against hitchhiking."

"Didn't know."

"The law seemed a good idea after a girl disappeared. I may have been the last person to see her. She was about where we're standing. Had on a shirt and jeans and thick shoes. A small backpack was on the ground. She was thumbing a ride. Most people don't remember. Sixty-nine. Eleven years ago. Hippie times. Her name was Haley Flagg."

"A student?"

"A dropout. What about you?"

"Four courses left before I have a degree in hand and no job."

"I'm Smith. Tim Smith, but I go by Smith." He glanced at the toolbox. "Anything in there I shouldn't see? Cannabis, for instance."

"Is that a problem?"

"I don't know where the Bower kids get it, but they get plenty."

Lenny introduced himself. They shook hands. Smith offered a ride to Prester. He moved a clipboard and paperwork for Lenny to sit in front. An air freshener dangled from the mirror. Smith said, "I usually patrol with a German shepherd, more for company than anything else. His day off. He's a bit fragrant."

Lenny told Smith the Thornes' address. One night he had stopped Maisie for speeding and no lights. "We try to be good neighbors. I didn't ticket her. Took her home. Mother was nice enough, but the daughter cussed me with some salty language. Claimed her VW was used and the speedo didn't work."

The Skylark was parked in the driveway. Smith was out of sight before Lia opened the door. Lenny explained his Jeep was laid up. He rattled his toolbox and told her he had washers left over from some other jobs.

"You're in charge," she said.

Lenny knelt under the sink and shut off the water. He took the faucet apart and replaced the old washer. His father had been a lobsterman. He advised Lenny to avoid the sea. Learn how to fix things with your hands. Other body parts can cause you trouble. Lenny was born a couple of months after he had married Lenny's mother.

Lenny reached under the sink again and turned on the water. He saw Maisie's feet before he saw the rest of her. "Put the plumbing in working order?"

"Think so," he said.

"Maybe you could do the same for me sometime." Her white shorts covered part of a tattoo. She inched them down enough for Lenny to see the rest of it. "A runic letter. It means a thorn tree." He didn't say anything, just admired how the ink contrasted with her skin.

"Show's over." She pulled up her shorts. Lenny turned on the water. No drips.

While Maisie toasted an English muffin, he used the kitchen phone to dial the number Warner had left him. After he hung up, Maisie asked who he had talked to.

"Mrs. Harrison. A house on the lake. A couple of rooms she wants painted."

"You know who her husband is?"

"My minor is art history. Zephyr Harrison teaches studio. Heard of him, but never met him."

"He has a reputation for painting nasty portraits."

"His wife said he doesn't do walls and ceilings."

Maisie poured herself a cup of coffee. "When will the Bug take to the highway again?"

"I'll check it out," Lenny said.

An hour later, with cash from Lia and the use of the Skylark, Lenny had purchased a new battery, tune-up parts for the Bug, and a kit to rebuild the Jeep's master cylinder. The NAPA store in Graham, the closest town to Prester, stocked what he needed, and he didn't have to drive to Burlington or Greensboro.

Vickie looked surprised. "You back." Lenny ordered a grilled cheese sandwich and a milkshake. "Big spender today."

She brought his shake. He stared at her satiny skin, glowing braids of black hair, deep eyes studying him. One more flirty white boy? He had never seen a woman like her in Maine.

"Want to swim?" he asked.

"Where? Dane Creek?"

"The lake."

"You allowed to go there?"

"My car has a sticker."

"*Your* car?"

"The car I'm driving. A lady let me borrow it."

"White lady?"

"Yes."

"She let me borrow her skin? Cause otherwise security would get me off the property faster than the devil seize your sinful soul." Vickie walked away and came back with Lenny's sandwich. "Pleased to be asked though."

"Ever been to the lake?"

"My mama cleaned a house there. Sometimes I'd help. I thought about dipping a toe in the water, but she say not to. The husband of the lady Mama worked for wanted to paint me. Mama said no. He painted girls without their clothes on."

"Mr. Harrison?"

"That's right. I guess he's important."

This time Vickie kept the extra Lenny gave her. Someone had left a note in the Skylark: *You won't get away with it.* He folded the note and tucked it into his pocket. He returned the Skylark and Lia drove him home.

"Ever hear of Haley Flagg?"

"Not for a while," Lia said. "A girl from a wealthy family who dropped out, camped in the woods." Lia pointed to the trees that grew close to the trailer. "She traded her designer outfits for peasant dresses from Goodwill. Sold her car too. The SBI and FBI have lists of missing people like her." Lia brushed her hand down Lenny's arm. "You might consider a trip to Goodwill yourself. To describe your clothes as shabby would be generous."

"I have a wardrobe for special occasions. Coat, tie, the works."

"Dress up and I'll take you to dinner. My treat. You choose."

"Oliver's."

"The most expensive place in the village."

"I work at the other one. I have a shift tonight."

"Oliver's then."

Late in the afternoon Warner stopped to ask if Lenny had found his note. He stayed to help bleed air out of the Jeep's brakes after Lenny had repaired the cylinder and filled it with fluid.

Lenny stood under the solar shower behind the trailer until the hot water ran out. He dressed in his Nook uniform—black trousers, white shirt, and black vest. Only six reservations on the book. At nine the manager told him to call it a night. Vickie was sitting on the trailer steps.

"Carleton," she said. "We was riding around, talking, sipping refreshment."

She pointed toward the trees. "Most of what's back there was Carleton's grandfather's homeplace. Carleton parked in what used to be the lane to the house. He got frisky. I wasn't in the mood. He left me and drove away." She fingered her torn shirt. "Preacher Daddy be waiting up. At least I got my bra back."

Lenny had a T-shirt that fit her. He looked away as she put it on. Hers smelled like jasmine. She didn't mind his smelled like sweat. She lifted herself into the Jeep. He was sweet, she said, and didn't say anything more until he stopped at a traffic light on College and she gave him directions to the south end of the village where many of the school's Black workers lived—cottages with sparse yards, chickens and gardens. A door opened. A man looked out. The door shut behind her. Lenny sensed a neighborhood holding its breath. White troublemakers drove Jeeps, four-wheeled where they wanted to, tore up lawns, and dreams.

❧

Lenny had pushed the Bug out of the garage. Maisie was going to help him. "She sleeps late," Lia said, her back to slim morning sun. She wore a thin dress and sandals. "What's the plan here?"

Lenny knelt behind the VW, looked up, and shaded his eyes. "Replace the battery, points, plugs, condenser. Check belts and hoses."

Lia pointed to a gauge beside his knee. "Compression," he said. "I'll need your help."

"I'm not going to get all dirty, am I?"

"You'll sit in the car and turn over the motor when I tell you."

By the time Lenny finished checking the cylinders, drops of rain spotted the driveway. He gathered his tools and stored them in the Jeep. Lia hadn't moved from the driver's seat. He ducked in beside her. Rain was falling harder.

"I grew up in Charlotte. My parents had money," she said. "I remember the Packards they drove when I was little. You could almost live in them. Nothing like this tinny German toy."

"It's reliable."

"They weren't.'

"The Packards?"

"My parents. When they died, they had spent almost everything and sold what was worth anything. I wouldn't have had a dime except for my grandmother. Being poor sucks."

"You're not poor now, are you?"

"Comfortably middle class, I suppose. After college I worked at Guthrie's, a broker on McDowell Street. He's dead now. Thomas was one of his clients. That's how we met. I knew something about investing from my grandfather, but what Guthrie profited from was what I learned from men who had known Guthrie when they were students together at the college. Three or four liked to spend weekends here away from wives and commitments. Guthrie suggested I might help them relive their golden schooldays, feel young again. They offered me advice and tips on the market for the pleasure of my company."

"What about Thomas?"

"Guthrie had clients all over the area, people with showy homes and properties. I was popular. Thomas accompanied me to lots of parties and events. They turned him on. One steamy night on the way back from a bash in Raleigh—I don't know if it was what I wore or how I smelled or the way I had flirted at the party or how much he'd had to drink—he couldn't wait until I was home in my apartment. He saw a motel and couldn't wait to get a room. He had me in the parking lot, my skirt hiked up, leaning over the fender of his Chevy.

"We married. I had Maisie. Guthrie didn't want me back. I wasn't glamorous anymore. What do you think?"

Rain drummed on the roof now. What did *he* think? He wasn't sure they could agree on the meaning of glamorous. She showed herself off. Her body held your attention. Her eyes sized you up. An invitation and warning—Lenny wasn't sure. "I don't think you're happy."

"Depends on what day it is. I have my friends. Thomas has his. I like the house to myself."

"Do your friends ever stay over?"

"My house, my rules. No."

Lenny couldn't see out anymore. Lia leaned past him and opened the glovebox.

"Looking for something?"

"A cigarette...and please, no lectures."

THE HARRISONS' HOUSE WAS CEDAR with vertical panels of glass. Mrs. Harrison—fifties, graying hair, bangs, brown eyes. She wore white slacks and a beige tunic. "Call me Miss M," she said.

They agreed on four dollars an hour. Today was the sixth. Zephyr (she called him Zeph) planned to deliver work to his gallery in Atlanta. He usually stayed a week. He disliked having strangers in the house. Could Lenny start next Monday? She'd already arranged for the paint. He could charge whatever he needed at Buck's.

Everyone called the pharmacist "Dr. Teddy." He sat down beside Lenny, who didn't recognize the woman behind the counter. "Nadine," Dr. Teddy said. She brought him a coffee and took Lenny's order. Vickie had called in sick. Only times she didn't show up was when Preacher Daddy kept her home. She was easily led into temptation.

"Wasn't you, was it?" Dr. Teddy asked.

"Why would you think so?"

"I have two Black employees, Vickie and Watson, who does the cleaning and tends the trash. I heard her tell him you asked her out."

"She's got a boyfriend."

"Carleton Pyle. Keep your distance. Or keep a weapon handy. He's not a nice person."

"Vickie must like him."

"She'll change her mind.

"Then maybe she'll go out with me."

"Both of you would regret it." Dr. Teddy left to fill a prescription.

❧

THE CAMPUS THE WAY LENNY LIKED IT: hum of bees, dusty light, stretches of lawn, islands of shade under the oaks and poplars, vistas of summer lingering, the solitude before students returned.

Two sand and gravel paths edged with boxwoods circle the fountain between Old Quad and New Quad. Here and there beds of sasanqua, groves of Osmanthus. In neoclassical style Mori (administration) and Monroe (registrar and records), the oldest buildings, rise from stone foundations aged green and mossy, the ocher bricks of the walls paling to yellow. The bell tower in the distance. Lenny had time to visit the registrar's office to make sure he was eligible to enroll fall term. He waited to speak with Sandy, chief officer of records and financial aid.

Lunch hour was just over. Two Prester traditions. One, noon swim when the male faculty have the outdoor pool to themselves and bathing suits are not permitted, a left-over from polio days when people believed germs multiplied in wool and cotton. Two, female faculty and staff ascend the bell tower to spy on the bathers from the observation deck. Sandy sat down, stowed a pair of binoculars in her desk drawer, and gave Lenny a sly smile.

"Got a favorite?"

"Roger Royal. Economics," she said.

She opened Lenny's file. With work-study he could enroll fall semester. She lowered her voice. "The athletic department needs tutors. There's pay and perks." He might even join faculty pool time. She leaned closer. "They want someone who can write. You won the English department's essay prize two years in a row."

"Write what?"

"The papers athletes are assigned."

"Cheat, you're saying?"

"Lenny, I'm merely mentioning an opportunity that pays well. Take it or leave it."

"Who do I see?"

"You're looking at her. But not today. Stay in touch."

❧

EACH FRESHMAN RECEIVES A BRIEF history of the college. In 1809, Caedmon Prester, a sturdy Presbyterian minister, arrived at a settlement in the Carolina wilderness and might not have stayed but his wagon was worn out from rough travel, as were his wife and three children. He undertook to school them and any others, old or young, who wished to learn letters and numbers. The settlement grew, and Caedmon called the one-room schoolhouse an academy.

The unofficial history suggests Caedmon was jovial and generous, fond of books, and enjoyed passing the afternoon sipping spirits and making up tall tales about converting Indians to Christendom. The residents decided to honor him by naming the community Prester. Eventually the academy was so named as well. Eventually, eventually the academy called itself a college, and eventually, eventually, eventually became one, admitting both men and women. It survived the 1860s and a hundred years later was one of the most prestigious private colleges in the South.

❦

Red's Books and News occupies a wedge of space on College Street between the movie theater and a shoe store. Red sells books heavy on sex and violence as well as the Raleigh *News & Observer* and *The Wall Street Journal*, but most customers are there to drink beer or browse the racks of magazines that cater to almost every sexual fantasy or pass the time exchanging opinions with Red, a bald stocky man with fierce brown eyes, whose favored topics are the stock market, local politics, and the general depravity of the human race. The business has survived several attempts by faculty wives to shut it down.

Four o'clock every afternoon, Cliff Barrow, a jowly six-footer with a trimmed beard, leans at the end of the bar, can of Budweiser in hand, in honor of Caedmon. Cliff graduated from the college, served in Vietnam, and writes a weekly feature—Cliff's Notes—for the *Village View*, published twice a week.

Lenny ordered a Coke. Cliff looked him up and down. "You know why the college's teams are called the Sweepers?" he asked.

"There was a broom factory here."

"1879 to 1946." Cliff took a long drink. "Prester's teams get swept a lot, especially basketball."

"I don't pay much attention."

"You're not the rah-rah type? More humdrum?"

"I prefer pay-as-you-go."

"Hmm." Another long drink. "Times they are a-changin'. Dylan got that right. So did Coach Bliss. I hear he recruited a couple of Black hotshots. One can pick two hundred pounds of cotton in the day and score thirty points at night."

"Impressive," Lenny said.

"What sort of academic skills you think he has?"

"Prester has high standards."

"Used to is what I'm saying."

Red was mixing something fizzy. "The college is going dark is what Cliff means."

Cliff continued, "Wallace Wallace is the man's name. Not sure about the other recruit's. Mr. Wallace is from rural Georgia. Just learning the ABCs was probably worthy of the honor roll."

Red and the customer with the fizzy drink laughed. Cliff noticed Lenny didn't. "I wrote President Bullard. I'm not the only alum who doesn't favor compromising the school's reputation by admitting unqualified athletes like Mr. Wallace."

Lenny said, "You haven't met him. You don't know he's not qualified."

"Of course, I do. The demographics tell the story."

"Maybe there's a subtext."

Cliff squeezed his empty beer can out of shape. "Lenny, you got the English-major lingo down. If you ever finish your degree, what are you going to do with it?"

"Teach somewhere. Middle school, maybe."

Red handed Cliff another beer. "You read my recent Note?"

"Not yet. What have I missed?"

"On one of my midnight prowls of College Street, I found a crocheted shoulder bag like the ones popular a few years ago.

It was lying on the bench in front of the cafeteria. It put me in mind of the student who disappeared, the Flagg girl. I know that old Airstream you inhabit is close to where she disappeared. Thought you'd be interested."

"You should read it," Red said, glancing at Lenny.

"I mailed Mr. Flagg a copy, the girl's father. He's interested. He's spent mucho dinero on private detectives trying to find her," Cliff said.

The man with the fizzy drink recalled Cliff's account of a naked woman one misty dawn riding a unicycle down College.

"She disappeared too," Cliff said. "But nothing criminal was suspected. Only that alcohol had skewed my vision and corrupted my imagination. She was stunning to behold."

The man finished his fizzy drink and wiped his mouth. "The Flagg girl was pretty too, wasn't she?"

"I heard that Harrison painted her," Cliff said. "His landscapes are mundane and academic, but his portraits of pets and children are surprising—sinister felines, salivating dogs, boys and girls looking like threats or tarts. Wonder how he portrayed Miss Flagg."

❧

Next day Lenny finished one room—first coat, walls and ceiling. Four thirty he drove to campus to ask Sandy how much the tutoring job paid and what were the perks. She gathered her purse and umbrella and followed him to the faculty parking lot, where he'd illegally parked. She said, "My throat's dry. If we're going to discuss what I think we are, I'll need lubrication. The Cat? I'll pay."

Sandy, almost sixty, spry and muscular, an avid tennis player, rumored to have carried on shamelessly with the tennis coach, which would have ended his marriage had not his heart given out on a recruiting trip. Jet black hair frames her face. Her eyes appear blue or green depending on the light.

The Cat—short for Catalonia—is a bistro on Orwell Street that features spirits and small-vintage wines selected by the owner on his travels. Décor: white wall, dark wood. Lighting: early summer evening in Barcelona. Music: distant guitar/ Segovia/ Bream. Prices: *muy caro*. Tapas available as well as an explanation of what they are.

A supple waitress with a long braid of auburn hair and dressed in a frilly white blouse, cummerbund, and impossibly tight legging brought Sandy's Polish vodka with a splash of pomegranate and a Meyer lemon twist along with Lenny's tempranillo reserva.

Although the room was almost empty, Sandy lowered her voice. The going rate for tutoring athletes was five dollars an hour. Getting someone's essay in shape to hand in might take several hours.

Lenny said, "I ran track. The guys I knew wrote their own papers."

"Track and swimming recruit for smarts. Their GPAs make the collective average for all Prester sports look good." The door opened. A wedge of five-thirty light peaked and faded across the floor. "Coach Bliss recruited two players he predicts will take Prester into postseason play. Long time since that happened. He's concerned one of them, Wallace Wallace, will have a hard time academically. He barely graduated from a way-the-hell-and-gone school in Georgia. Bliss says he can shoot the eyes out of the basket and pick three hundred pounds of cotton a day."

Lenny sighed. That was a hundred pounds more than Cliff gave him credit for. "Too bad we don't offer a class in that."

"Don't joke about it. You would be assigned full time to Mr. Wallace."

Lenny savored his wine. "Very good," he said.

"And very pricey."

Lenny heard the message: I'm treating you because we're making a deal here. Don't let me down. "Perks?" he asked.

"Office space. Varsity weight room. Secretarial help. Noon swim."

They finished their drinks. Sandy paid. Outside, she rubbed her arms. "You can feel summer taking its leave," she said and lowered herself into her car. "You on board?"

Lenny said he was. They shook hands. He asked about the car. Sixty-seven MG, acquired used from a dealer in Burlington.

LENNY WAS ABOUT TO SPREAD a drop cloth and start painting the ceiling of the second room. After lunch he'd give another coat to the walls of the first room. He could hear Miss M talking on the kitchen phone—something about a painting the caller considered unshowable and wouldn't pay for.

Finished with the ceiling, Lenny sat on the lawn close to the shore. A crow perched on the roof of the nearby shed where Zephyr stored tools and lawn equipment and eyed Lenny eating his lunch—peanut butter sandwich, apple, and a Sprite. Miss M sat down beside him and lit a cigarette.

"Zeph hates me smoking in the house, even when he's traveling." She exhaled and watched the smoke swirl and disappear. "I put up with studio smells and have to listen to clients like the one today. You'd think he could get along with a cigarette or two now and then. A pack lasts me a whole month. I need a smoke and a tall alcoholic drink. Could you hear me?"

"I heard the word *obscene*."

"So did I. Several times. The portrait provokes, but it's not obscene, it's..." Miss M watched the smoke drift away. "Mrs. Cardwell is married to the college's attorney. He's fifty, she's younger. Big house east of town. She gardens. He has a putting green. Spends his spare time practicing, practicing. To his credit, he adores Marsha—Mrs. Caldwell. He commissioned Zeph to paint her portrait. I'll show you."

Lenny followed Miss M down a tiled hall to the studio, which took up nearly a quarter of the house. There wasn't the chaos of jars and tubes of paint, brushes and rags, rolls of paper, stretchers and canvas that he expected.

"Zeph compensates for his insecurities by surrounding himself with order." She pointed to the painting displayed on an easel in the corner of the room. "I give you Marsha."

Tanned face, hazel eyes, one brow raised, quizzical smile, Marsha sat on a chair in a garden. She wore a filmy white dress buttoned to her throat, the suggestion of primness undone by the dress being lifted above the wearer's open thighs between which rested a basket of black-eyed Susans. The trees rose and curved and shaped space into a frame, a niche sheltering Marsha.

Miss M said, "Zeph considers the work charming. Mr. Caldwell violently disagrees."

"Her dress would be modest except the way it's hiked up." Lenny bent closer. "No underwear. You can see her breasts."

"One of Zeph's motifs. What else?"

"The choice of flowers and where the basket is must mean something."

"Marsha and Susan Miller, who manages the college's food service, spend lots of time together, their own version of naked noon exercise, according to gossip. I always think rumors abound in college towns more than other places."

Lenny stood back and fingered the shape of the niche in the air but didn't say anything.

"Don't be shy. What are you thinking?"

"Something anatomical."

"The suggestion of a vulva?"

"Yes."

"You're blushing. Still a lot of boy in you."

"What's going to happen? To the painting, I mean."

"Zeph will store it with the others and keep part of the commission and forget about the rest."

"Others?"

"Commissions that didn't work out. Portraits of young adults that their parents objected to. One boy is too sulky and couldn't Zeph cover up the kid's bad skin? Another, My son should be wearing a suit, not jeans and a T-shirt. Or, You made my daughter look like a slut—she's falling out of her dress. Then there's the dreamy nude musing over her reflection in the lake. She disappeared. Zeph considered telling her father about the painting, but he worried how he would feel about his daughter posing nude and the possibility that someone abducted her and did one thing have anything to do with the other. He doubted he could convince anyone that the girl chose the pose herself and paid Zeph to paint her. He doesn't really like the piece, but he keeps it in case she's alive and wants what she paid for."

Lenny followed Miss M to the kitchen. "People consider Zeph rude and opinionated, and he is, but he's not unkind, and he's oddly sentimental. He talks to Haley. I've heard him."

"Haley Flagg?"

"Yes, the poor girl he painted. He imagines her life, what she was thinking, staring at her reflection. He speculates why she wanted to be naked and why she never collected the painting and why she sold her possessions and took to living in the woods."

❧

An evening at Oliver's: Supper for two, plus cocktails and wine, around $150, depending on the wine. In the short time since the county voted to permit sales of liquor by the drink, the selection of alcoholic beverages had gone from poor to excellent, predictable to almost exotic.

Lia ordered two of Oliver's special bourbons, hers with a dash of bitters, no ice. She raised her glass. "Highlight of my day, being out with you. Otherwise, it's been a downer. Thomas is on his way home."

Prawns arrived, along with a rather sweet Italian white, compliments of the house. Next came Lenny's lobster, which waited while the server deboned Lia's Dover sole. The sommelier scowled while Lenny appraised the Graves.

Passing the table, other dinners appraised him, looking as presentable as possible in his dress-up clothes that some widow had contributed to Goodwill so he could look couth. His wool jacket was conspicuously out of season among the summer-weight seersuckers, poplins, and linens. One swarthy man with gold jewelry stopped to comment on Lia's lovely dress. He dallied at other tables too, kissing cheeks, shaking hands. Mr. Weaver, Lia said. The mayor. Every time Lenny glanced at a man seated close by, he was staring at Lia.

After crème brûlées, Port, and coffee, Lia drove home. "You are staying for a swim, aren't you?"

Lenny's mother preached that life is generous with pain, stingy with pleasure. When it's offered, take it. She had pinched his cheek and said, but you never listen. When the party is getting started, you always have an excuse to call it a night. No wonder he didn't have friends.

Alcohol had emptied Lenny's mind of excuses. "Your house, your rules," he said.

The cabana was walled with mirrors. Lenny's mother appeared again. How happy he must be to see himself everywhere, always so prideful and aloof, the family brain who read books, used fancy words, and aimed for an Ivy league college. If he wanted friends, he should drink beer and talk about getting laid like other kids did.

Lenny relieved himself and took his time undressing. Lia was already in the pool, buoyed in the blueish shimmer of underwater lights. He lowered himself into the water—soft, warm, and clean, not seething, salty, and cold like the sea in which he had learned to swim, or at least to tread water, slapping at the waves, gasping for air.

He floated. Lia swam under him. He stood up and tried to remember the names of constellations. Lia surfaced behind him, pressing her breasts against his back, palms sliding and circling down his thighs.

"I see you're busy," a voice said.

By the time Lia was out of the pool, the man who had stared at her at dinner was gone. A few minutes later, so was Lenny.

❧

Miss M opened the door and looked at her watch. Lenny promised to finish the second room before the end of the day. "Zeph's here," she said. He may say hello, or he might ignore you entirely."

Lenny got to work. From time to time, he heard distant voices. Otherwise, the house was quiet until he heard a throat cleared behind him.

"Name one goddamn painting you like."

Tall and blue-eyed, gray hair hanging to his shoulders, Zephyr Harrison wore black dungarees, a gray polo shirt, and loafers that looked expensive. Alligator? Lenny had seen a pair like them in a shop window on Hawthorne Street.

"Manet's *Bar at the Folies Bergère*," he said.

"The tricky perspective, that's what attracts you?"

"The girl."

"Suzon was her name. What about her?"

"Sadness."

"If I had guessed which Manet you'd pick, I would have said his *Olympia*."

"Spoiled women don't appeal to me."

Zephyr thought a moment. "The black cat in the painting—*La Chatte*. I assume you understand what it refers to."

"I think I do."

"Then no comment from me is required. What's your hourly rate?"

"Four dollars." Lenny inquired how much Zephyr charged to paint someone's portrait. Lenny's mother complained he was abrupt and rude and asked too many questions.

Zephyr answered, "A lot or almost nothing, which is why so many parents hire me to immortalize their offspring. Oil on canvas instead of a photograph. I want the work regardless of what the client can pay."

"I understand some don't."

"It happens. I'm not fond of adolescents or house pets. Too often I sexualize the former and portray the latent savagery of the latter." Zephyr shrugged. "But sometimes I fall in love and the work disappoints. I don't...well...I've said enough. You need to finish your work, and I need to deal with a hostile father who feels I have maligned his tender daughter by depicting her seated before a boudoir mirror, brushing her golden tresses. The parent objects to the way her shirt is carelessly open, revealing too much breast, and the way her leg is casually bent, revealing too much thigh. It does no good to assure him that the choice was hers. I merely made suggestions. She made herself comfortable. I require hours of sitting. Comfort is important. With animals I work from photographs.

"In any event, she's sixteen and capable of deciding for herself. If Daddy wanted prim purity and the sloe-eyed family spaniel, he should have commissioned someone else. Or had a different daughter. The way he attacked me, you'd think I was Balthus. If you want adolescent nudity, he's your man." Zephyr snickered. "Lots of cats in his work."

Lenny finished and Miss M paid him. He was too thin, she said and handed him a bag of muffins she had baked that afternoon. At home, he put them in the refrigerator next to the box of Wheaties, which he kept there away from mice. He heard the crush of gravel. The man got out of a green Volvo and kicked one of the cans Lenny hadn't picked up. "The bears have my number," Lenny said. "I bag my trash. They unbag it."

"Humans. I'd suspect the McGoon sisters, Deb and Donna, my nieces. They like playing jokes."

"What can I help you with?"

"Warner spoke of you. I thought I should introduce myself." The man reached out his hand. "Wade DeFoe. I'm president of the Bower Residents' Association."

"Tanner's father?"

"You know Tanner?"

"Mrs. Thorne mentioned him."

"My son can be a handful. So can Lia. I heard she paid for supper at Oliver's. She's usually not so public. How old are you?"

"Twenty-five next month."

"Lia is a tease. She craves reassurance. She plays easy to get, but she's untouchable."

"What's that mean?"

"I hope you don't find out."

Sandy told Lenny about the meeting. Four o'clock, Newell Gym conference room at the end of an echoing hall: displays of deflated balls inked with scores, torn gloves, faded autographs, stained jerseys, nets, tarnished cups and plaques. The floor of the basketball arena had recently been refreshed. The pungent smell of varnish spoiled the air.

Four men Lenny didn't recognize (except for the math whiz who had graduated the previous June), a few younger faculty, and several coaches sat around an oval table. A brawny man in shirtsleeves pointed Lenny to an empty chair and introduced himself—Arthur Hilton, sports science and coordinator of the tutorial program. His neck was thicker than Lenny's thigh. He named each coach and their sport, each faculty member and their subject. The tutors (four plus Lenny) remained anonymous. "Never forget," he said, "you cannot do someone's assignment for them. Remember the honor code. The work they hand in must be their own, not yours. Cheating will not be rewarded or tolerated." He turned to Coach Bliss. "How did Shakespeare put it? 'Down that road madness lies'?"

Bliss stared blankly back. Hilton thanked everyone for attending. In the hallway Bliss shook Lenny's hand. Six nine and thin, students called him Spider. "Sandy gave me a rundown on you. Did Hilton say it right, the quotation?"

"It's 'That way madness lies.'"

Bliss pointed down the hall. "This way my office lies."

It was remarkably free of photographs, posters, or memorabilia. Desk, three chairs, filing cabinet, lamps, coat rack, a small table. "I'm not big on decorating," Bliss said. "Those shelves, those books and binders are years of rules and regulations. I go by one rule—winning. I have a talented bunch this season. Sandy probably mentioned Wallace Wallace. She assured me I can count on you to keep him eligible. You'll be assigned some others, but WW is your prime responsibility. He's Black, he and Tyrone Taylor. Tyrone won't be a problem.

I can pay you five-fifty, which is more than the others are making."

Bliss retrieved an old Polaroid from his desk and took a photo of Lenny to post in the athletic office so the lifeguard and staff would know Lenny had permission to join noon swim as well as use the varsity weight room (carpeted and full of shiny equipment) and the restricted lockers and showers. Lenny's "office" was one of several cubicles, each with two chairs, a worktable, a bookcase, and an overhead florescent light.

At home Lenny changed into his Nook outfit. The restaurant filled up, a cheerful crowd, mostly faculty in a jovial, post-summer mood. Professor Thorne had reserved a table by the window. He said he remembered Lenny, who recited the specials and recommended several wines. Juan, the busser, gave Maisie a long looking over. His brother, the elegant but mute Carlito, recently arrived on the boatlift from Cuba, gave her another. Lia appeared exhausted, Maisie bored, Thomas distracted.

Lenny was home by eleven, asleep by twelve, awake again by one. Maisie lay beside him.

"You should lock your door."

"Lock's broken," he said.

"Get a bigger bed."

"Where would I put it?"

"You need to put me somewhere."

"Not here."

She nestled her cheek against his. "We were drinking. Warner kicked us off the beach. He probably radioed Smith. No DUIs, if you please."

Lenny said he would drive her home. Except in winter, he

slept naked. He lifted the sheet, climbed over her, and gathered his clothes.

"Sweet butt," she said.

"Look but don't touch."

"Because you're so precious? Or don't you think I can afford you?"

"I'm cheap."

"I'm not," she said.

Smith's cruiser was parked up the road. A couple of miles, he and deputy dog followed them, then turned away. Maisie had left her wallet and keys in her VW parked in Lenny's yard. He helped her find the spare house key under the garden urn in the circle of liriope near the front door.

Two thirty. Home again. At first he didn't notice the bracelet on his pillow, a circle of silver links with the letters L M T, a heart, and L M T again. He put the bracelet in a drawer and undressed.

❧

REGISTRATION DAY. LENNY SIGNED UP for two courses: American Regional Art and Major American Novels.

Wallace Wallace, six-five, one-hundred-eighty pounds, was waiting in Bliss's office. He introduced Lenny to Wallace. "Hey," Wallace said, then looked down as if inspecting his scuffed leather shoes. Lenny opened Wallace's registration packet. Twelve hours: Math A, remedial English, Games and Sports. "That's new this year," Bliss said. "You trace how kicking some poor devil's skull around an ancient town in Italy became soccer. Stuff like that."

Wallace said he could calculate okay, but writing was a chore. "Ain't read much. Don't have a lot of words. Got a smooth jump shot, though."

Official practices wouldn't begin for several weeks, but every afternoon the team would meet unofficially for conditioning and pick-up games. Wallace and Lenny would meet twice a week to discuss how things were going.

⁂

NOON SWIM. LENNY HESITATED before opening the door from the locker room and stepping into the sunlight. He eased the door closed and dropped his towel on the cement deck. A dozen faculty sprawled poolside, reading or lounging in the sun. Others swam back and forth in lanes marked by white ropes bobbing on the blue water. Seated in a tall chair, the lifeguard glanced at Lenny, then looked back at the swimmers.

The sign warned No Diving. Lenny inched down the ladder. The water was warm and pungent with chlorine. In the distance the bell tower loomed. Figures appeared on the observation platform, but he couldn't make out who they were. A pulse of light flashed off someone's binoculars. He swam to the opposite end and back and climbed out.

Zephyr Harrison startled Lenny. "Thought it was you. What are you teaching that lets you intrude on our congregation?"

"Tutoring, sir, not teaching."

"I noticed you signed up for Graves's Woodwork course?"

"Woodwork?"

"Grant Wood, he and Benton and the other regionalists."

"You disapprove?"

"Not at all. One day they'll be rediscovered." Harrison took Lenny by the shoulders and turned him around. "The man roiling lane two is Professor Royal. We call him Beefcake. Terrific specimen." Harrison pointed to the bell tower. "This is what they're up there waiting for—Beefcake, full frontal. I think his image is burned into their retinas. Cézanne would have loved him. Eakins even more."

Lenny showered and dressed and then walked to his car. The Skylark was parked in his yard. Lia was sitting on the trailer steps.

"For all the good it did, we grounded her," Lia said. "Of course, her friends will drive her anywhere she wants to go. She did find an apartment, a sublet above the drugstore. Cliff Barrow lives across the hall. Wonder if the two of them will get along. Cliff can be nosy and judgmental."

"Were you waiting for me?"

"I wanted to apologize for Maisie's behavior and thank you for getting her home again. Hope you don't mind having her car as yard art for a few days."

"Glad to help."

"Glad about anything else?"

"School's starting. Fine weather. In a few minutes I'm going for a run. Got a pizza to heat for supper."

"Maisie said she crawled into bed with you."

"*Onto* not into."

"She came home missing an item of underwear."

"You want to look around?"

"I already did. Found a woman's shirt. Jasmine isn't my favorite scent. You know you should really lock your door."

"I don't want to discourage visitors."

"I appreciate your humor. What I wouldn't appreciate is Maisie showing up again and having sex with you." Lia caressed Lenny's face. "I saw you first."

Half an hour later he was sprinting toward the beach parking lot. Warner was picking up trash on the roadside.

"Wears me out watching you." He coughed and spit. "Fortunately, I haven't needed to chase any miscreants lately. Thorne girl and the boy were drinking. I sent her home. Smitty saw her in your car. Guess she got to your place and switched horses."

Warner coughed again and patted Lenny's shoulder. "Got a job for you—night work. Interested?" Lenny said he was. "Several residents claim they've seen a figure cross the road and disappear up the hillside. Draper's dog never barks, but the other night it took off yapping after someone or something. Mr. Tittle reported someone swiped two cans of soda from the fridge in his garage. The man keeps count of everything. Also, he found traces of dirt on the carpet of his Caddy and thinks someone with muddy shoes snoozed in the backseat. Make your own schedule. Mr. DeFoe authorized me to pay you ten an hour."

"Sounds good," Lenny said.

My refuge was the Hotel Azul, the blue hotel. The walls were actually painted white, and the windows close to the street had bars on them. There were Mayan ruins nearby and lots of tourists, who spent lots of money because pesos didn't feel like real money to them, and most things were cheap—especially women and tequila. Mushrooms and marijuana were easy to come by.

By the time I arrived in the Yucatan, Inez had blown through the year before. The commune I expected to join was gone, their property flooded by Inez, then plundered by local gangs. Guards carrying automatic weapons and walkie-talkies protected the pricey beach resorts farther down the coast.

The hotel catered to tourists. My high school French was passable. My Spanish was improving. Ernesto, the manager, known as Dobo, hired me "for my tongue." You know, you speak to foreigners, he said. Make them understand. I understood perfectly well the sexual innuendo.

Hippies and gentuza (riffraff) he called the people I had intended to meet. All gone, he said and arranged for me to occupy a linen closet converted into the slim room on the fourth floor. When the elevator worked, it stopped on the third. The fourth was mostly storage. I had a window, though. Nights I could see up at the stars or down at the putas *and their customers in the alley that connected Fifth Avenue, the main street, with the area of shacks and trailers where most of the hotel employees lived and the putas provided what they were paid for. In the daytime a young man with a mottled iguana sat at a table, selling raffle tickets and taking bets on cockfights and other sports.*

Dobo paid me when he could, but my drinks and meals were free. I got by on the occasional tip from someone I had helped buy weavings or ceramics at "special" prices from the street vendors, who set up on Fifth Avenue and sold everything from local crafts and Cuban cigars to Chinese herbs and goat weed that promised to increase sexual potency. You could smoke the former after enjoying the benefits of the latter. The herbs, of course, were local too, and the special prices were what the vendors would gladly accept after I did my act and talked them down from the exaggerated prices they advertised. You get along real fine with them, Dobo complimented me. In return some vendors brought me tacos or tortillas and once a live chicken that I handed over to Hector, the hotel cook, and another time a bottle of local whiskey that burned my throat and turned my stomach, but Dobo liked it well enough.

Only once did he inquire about my life. The places I named had no meaning for him. His knowledge of U.S. geography consisted of Texas, Miami, and New York. I said my mother had died in an auto accident. My father was alive. He owned a factory that made stuff. I didn't tell him about the rest.

II

Lenny and Wallace sat on the low stone wall that separated the sidewalk from a cemetery on the far side of the gym. He liked his teammates. His classroom presence caused people to stare at him, respectfully, he thought. The student newspaper, *The Sweeper*, had published a preview of fall sports, which featured basketball and the freshmen recruits, which featured Wallace. Respect? Lenny wasn't so sure, but he kept his doubts to himself. Wallace complained that the chairs were too small for his body.

Only shrubs and random stones, no markers, who was buried behind them, Wallace asked. Slaves, Lenny told him. No one knew their names. The wall had recently been built to keep students and fans from parking cars on the dead.

Wallace looked down and thought awhile. "The professor, he assigned us to write a paper about something important that happen to us."

"Which professor?"

"Fleck."

Nicely planned, Lenny thought. Oswald Fleck was near retirement and had little interest in teaching anymore. He occupied space, did what he had to do, which was as little as possible. He preferred remedial English because it involved fewer writing assignments than English I or advanced courses. To disguise his indifference, he performed with old-school charm and a particular courtliness toward women—"our coeds" as he referred to them—many of whom found his courtesy condescending, as if mastering the comma splice or the difference between *lie* and *lay* was an intolerable offense to the feminine mind, which should be occupied with dress, manners, and marriage.

Lenny asked Wallace what he had written so far.

"I."

"I what?"

"I, that's all."

"What does 'I' want to write about?"

"Me, my sister, and the snake."

One summer morning Wallace had looked down from the loft where he and his brother slept and saw a rattlesnake coiled in his sister's crib near the fireplace of the family's cabin. Whenever the snake quivered and rattled its tail, she cooed and laughed. Wallace's parents were outside doing chores. He crept downstairs and while the snake curved and bobbed and shook it tail, he grabbed the snake behind its head and threw it outside. His brother shot the snake with the gun his parents kept under their bed. Later the brothers tried to imitate the rattling sound and coax their sister to laugh again, but she stared at them sadly until they stopped.

Lenny handed Wallace a notebook and pencil. "Write your first sentence."

Wallace wrote *I seen the snake* and gave the notebook to

Lenny. He crossed out *seen* and wrote *saw* and asked Wallace to describe the snake. An hour later Wallace had written two paragraphs describing the cabin, his sister, the snake, and dispatching it. "These stones hurt my butt," he said and stood up. "We finished?"

"You haven't written why what happened was important to you."

"The snake could have bit my sister and she die."

"Yes, but did you learn anything about yourself or how you feel about her or your family? Anything like that?"

"What you mean?"

"Were you surprised you could snatch something quick and heavy and deadly and throw it outside? I don't think I could."

"You could if you didn't think about it."

"Ah."

"Ah what?"

"Sometimes you shouldn't think? Sometimes thinking gets in the way?"

Wallace shrugged. "Guess I got to think about it."

"Let's celebrate your first paycheck," Sandy said.

The Cat was almost empty. They sat at the bar, and Lenny ordered a pricey oloroso.

Sandy said, "The other afternoon my car was three spaces from where I parked in the morning. The campus police suggested it was a joke or a prank. Someone in my office lifted the keys from my purse."

"What's the joke?"

"You tell me. Besides, I keep my purse in my bottom desk drawer. No one came near my desk all day."

"Any damage to the car?"

"None, but it was driven some. I watch the gas gauge carefully. Its mpg rating is dismal." Sandy finished her drink. "What do you think?"

"Someone hot-wired your car or has a key."

"Which would you bet on?"

"Hot-wire. Your car would be easy."

"Any advice?"

"Lock it, and don't leave the top down."

"That's what the cops said. I might mention what happened to Cliff Barrow. He'd be more interested than they were. The car originally belonged to Haley Flagg. You've heard about her?"

For supper Lenny fried a hamburger and heated a jar of beans. He read until eleven, then put on a black warm-up suit left over from his track-team days, drove to the lake, and parked behind the utility hut that Warner used as an office.

The lots were wide and deep and those that didn't border on the lake extended into the hillsides, more space than Lenny had expected for someone to hide. Occasionally a dog barked or car lights flickered and disappeared. Otherwise, he was alone. Two hours later he went home.

Maisie had been ungrounded. Friends have driven her to Lenny's to retrieve her car. She sat on the trailer steps, beer in hand. She wore an orange nylon jacket. Her black tights accentuated her long legs and sturdy thighs. Her hair was cut short now and bleached white as snow. She pointed to the cooler by her feet. "I planned to mellow you out, but you weren't here—prowling somewhere in your cat-burglar outfit I assume from the way you're dressed. I decided to mellow myself."

"Do I need to drive you again?"

"Not tonight."

"Anything else?"

"Wallace Wallace, know anything about him?"

"He plays basketball."

"I was walking on Old Quad. He was standing by a bush with flowers on it. He asked me if I knew what it was called. Maybe Lois, I said." Maisie looked at Lenny. "You're supposed to laugh."

"Did *he*?"

"He's a bit cautious in the humor department. He told me his name. We walked a while. He said he was a dumb jock."

"He plays basketball. He's not dumb."

"He mentioned having a tutor—you."

"That's accurate."

"He asked me about the school's social life, what students did and where they did it. I said I was a transfer from Colorado and would have to find out myself."

"I'm sure Prester isn't too different from where you were before."

"He asked if there were many Black students there and if white students would party with them. I said they would."

"Perhaps he had partying with you in mind."

"He said right now practices were open and I could watch him."

"Are you interested in basketball?"

"Not especially, but Wallace interests me."

"It's late," Lenny said.

"I'd stay but your accommodations are more suited for singles than doubles. However, my apartment has plenty of space."

Maisie left her empty Coors bottle on the steps, picked up the cooler, and kissed Lenny's cheek. "Keep me in mind." Halfway to her car, she turned around. "Your sheets don't smell good."

Vickie's shirt wasn't on the dresser where Lenny had left it. He undressed and lay down. Maisie was right. The pillow smelled. The sheets did too. In the morning he bundled them together and drove to town. Bailey's Laundromat on Cobb Street, a block from campus, opened at seven. At 7:10 Helen Bailey was loading the row of washers with the laundry students had dropped off in baskets and bags the day before. Seventy, wrinkled, and shaped like a gourd, Helen usually had a cigarette in the corner of her tiny mouth. Until 5:30 she held off opening the bottle of whiskey she stashed on a shelf in the narrow closet where she stored brooms and mops. She closed at six and started the five-minute walk to her apartment. In the past Lenny had helped her replace machines and hoses. She shared whiskey with him, whiskey and gossip. Some lipstick is harder to wash out than others, she said. Some of the smears weren't where you might expect to find them.

Helen sniffed Lenny's sheets. "You sleeping with vagrants or give up on personal hygiene?"

"It's a mystery," he said.

"No, it's not. One human being who disdains soap and water laid his or her sour body in your bed and took a siesta."

Helen stuffed the sheets into a washer. "Be ready at five. Bring your thirst. I always have mine with me."

Hilton had told Lenny he should make himself available to any student athlete who needed help with their writing. Besides Wallace Wallace, Lenny was assigned a sophomore Canadian soccer player, two junior Puerto Rican tennis players, and a pair of first-year Asian swimmers. He spent two hours in the library going over drafts of written work they had left for him to read before they met prior to practices in the early afternoon. The rest of the morning he spent in class.

❧

THE NOON RUSH AT THE drugstore counter had cleared out. Vickie mixed Lenny a second Coke while he ate his grilled cheese. "For someone who runs a lot, you don't eat healthy," she said.

"Used to run a lot."

"That basketball player was in here. The one whose parents named him the same thing twice. You know who I mean?"

"Wallace Wallace?"

"Yeah, he asked me what I did for fun. Worked, I said. He suggested we meet at Lindy's. The roast beef is tasty. I told him I went there once and people stared at me. Not nice stares either. He said people stare at him all the time. Big as he is, I guess they would. Big and Black. Compared to him, I could almost pass for white. I told him I had a boyfriend. We went up to them woods again where his granddaddy lived. Someone had gathered branches and made a place to lay down. Wasn't you, was it?"

"I failed Boy Scouts."

"You still got my shirt?"

"Somebody stole it. Could you bring me another?"

"Wear one and you take it off?"

"Like you said, you have a boyfriend."

"He doesn't own me."

"Am I to think I should keep on asking?"

"College boys tend to think too much."

❧

LENNY MET WITH THE TENNIS PLAYERS. Their one-page summaries of a Didion essay assigned in their contemporary literature class were thoughtful. Their use of commas and apostrophes needed improvement. They glanced at each other and commented in Spanish. Lenny didn't understand the words, but he sensed they weren't compliments.

He retrieved his sheets. Helen wouldn't let him pay. He walked her home and stayed for one drink of smooth and smoky bourbon, a gift from a professor who appreciated someone who didn't wash and tell.

She told him to drive carefully. He started down the hill to the trailer and saw Zephyr standing by his car on the roadside path overgrown with honeysuckle, dogfennel, and pokeweed that led to Carleton's grandfather's property. Lenny stopped and got out.

"An early evening like this, summer ending, the melancholy light, the smells, the silence…" Zephyr shook his head. "Haley occupies my mind. Here is about the last place anyone saw her. I hike to where a homestead used to be. Black family. Raised chickens and goats. The old man died. His children had better things to do. They never paid their taxes. There were wrangles about ownership. Squatters came and went. The house had walls, but the roof had fallen in. People made off with what they could. White kids used to meet for sex. Hot sex, I guess. A fire started and burned itself out, taking the walls and a few trees with it. The goat shed had long ago rotted away.

"Haley was last seen thumbing a ride and never seen again. At first people assumed whoever picked her up harmed her. Later some suggested a drifter camping at the old house killed her. Law enforcement has searched and found clothes and stuff, but nothing of Haley's. Plenty of animal remains, no human ones."

"What do *you* think?"

"Kids used to hitch rides. Haley's not the only one who went missing. She had sold or given away everything she owned, whatever marked her as a child of privilege. She wanted to disappear from one life into another—a commune somewhere, a sanctuary where people thrived on fruits and vegetables and loved each other. All were welcome." He shook his head. "A human Petri dish for food poisoning, dysentery, and chlamydia."

"She might have found what she was looking for, changed her name, and still be alive."

"I see her car, the one that woman—Sandy—drives. It spooks me. I remember Haley driving it, the wind in her hair, her smile." He shrugged. "Anyway, thanks for stopping. When I have a free afternoon, I'll show you her portrait."

It was dark now. At home Lenny reminded himself he needed to put a lock on his door.

Autumn arrived. Brisk mornings. Lenny would run his lake route, stopping at Warner's office to report seeing plenty of deer but no mysterious strangers lurking in the Bower.

Maisie appeared in Lenny's cubicle. "I overheard one of those Asian cuties you tutor giggling about your kissable mouth."

"Giggling is her second language."

"Personally, I go for your curly red hair and pale blue eyes. The worried frown I can do without."

"You need help?"

"Since official practices started, spectators aren't allowed." Maisie leaned over. Had she stopped wearing bras or only when she wanted a favor? "Can you snag me a press pass or something?"

"Ask the coach. Or Cliff, your neighbor. He works for the paper."

"He's weird. At midnight I'll hear him click-clacking on his typewriter, or I'll be coming back from Boxer's and he'll be walking up and down College Street, mumbling to himself. The other night I heard him say 'I know you're here.'"

"What's Boxer's?"

"A club on Potter Street. Opened in September. Folk Wednesday, Thursday; jazz Friday, Saturday."

Maisie reached into her jacket for a package of cigarettes.

"Let's go outside," Lenny said.

A paper cup scuttled hollowly across the asphalt. She lit a cigarette and hunkered down by the wall where Wallace preferred to have his tutorials instead of the cubicle.

"Wallace is something to watch," she said.

"Is he *something* at anything else?"

"I'm working on finding out."

Sometimes Dobo encouraged me to contact my family so they would know I was okay and wouldn't worry about me. Pen in hand, relocated to Mexico, think I'll stay, I would write. I tried to imagine the two of them, my father and stepmother, passing the letter back and forth as if the ink would fade and their assumption would return: I was missing and presumed dead.

And I was dead, at least to them. Sitting in the library, with solemn faces and highballs in hand, they would revise my father's estate plan. My brother would receive my share. Then the new maid in her starched outfit would announce dinner was served. Stepmother would lament that my not being there unbalanced the seating arrangement. Father would remark, Well, she never did fit in, did she? She never saw things the way we did. Which meant I had turned my back on the system that had provided abundant food, clothing, and palatial shelter as well as an excellent education. I could speak usable French and understood a bit of German, but the language of the women who worked the mills that made the garments that brought in the money that paid for the house that my father built was foreign to me. The words of the putas drifting up on the night air were far more understandable than the gestures of emptiness and resignation that comprised the vocabulary of the women my father employed and with whom he had his way far more brutally than in any transaction occurring in the alley under my window.

I assured Dobo that the possibility I might someday reappear, which meant as well I might not, was more a comfort to my family than a letter making known I was alive, which would only diminish the possibility I was out of their lives forever. With my Spanish and his English, I don't believe he understood, but he smiled and shrugged and patted my ass, which was another subject. If I'd let him do more, a room with a bigger bed was available.

III

Wallace and Lenny met in his cubicle now. If Wallace held out his arms, he could touch both walls at the same time.

"Professor Fleck, he gets in my face about the way I talk in class. When I open my mouth, I sound like I never passed first grade. I wanted to tell him the schoolhouse I started at didn't have grades, only Miss Curdy taking turns with each of us, filling our heads with the alphabet and stuff. Wasn't until the yellow bus carried us to town and we sat at desks in a big room in a brick building that we were put in grades."

"What does Fleck say about your writing?"

"Improving, but he knows you been helping me put a little shine on my words and straightening out my verbs and tenses. Like you call it, polishing my prose."

Lenny hoped Hilton didn't suspect he was doing too much polishing. "Practice going okay?"

"Ol' Bliss is tough. Never heard a coach cuss so much, but the team's good. We're going to win plenty of games."

"What about your social life?"

"Miss Vickie—you know, the one from the drugstore—Sunday afternoon we went fishing."

"Fishing?"

"Her boyfriend didn't much like it, but her daddy said fishing was a holy activity for a Sunday afternoon. Jesus fished."

"Where did you go?" Lenny asked.

"Dane Creek, down behind a trailer park. I thought that lake I heard about would be a better place to catch something, but Miss Vickie warned me I catch hell going there."

"Did you catch anything?"

"Mr. Lenny, we spent most time joking and fooling around and wiggling our lines in the water. If I had hooked something, Miss Maisie warned me not to eat it. She claimed some of them trailers straight piped nasty stuff into the creek."

"When do you see her?"

"After practice. She's there a couple of times a week. She got a pass—*credential*, she calls it. A favor from someone she knows at the *Village View*. I learned that's a newspaper. She sits way up in the stands, doesn't bother anybody."

"Don't you have an important writing assignment due soon?"

"The book report." Wallace reached into backpack and held up a battered copy of *The Old Man and the Sea*. "So far, I read half."

Lenny checked Fleck's assignment schedule. The report was due a week after the first game. Wallace pushed the book into his pack and slung it over his shoulder. "Got to go," he said. "Man from the paper, he goin' to interview me, take my picture."

"What's his name?"

"Burrow...Borrow...something like that. Could be the person who gave Maisie the pass. I'll try to speak good so he write good things about me."

Late afternoon Lenny knew Wallace would be the topic of conversation at Red's. A student lingered in the rear of the store, browsing the periodicals featuring busty Latinas, paying no attention to Cliff in his customary corner or Red behind the counter. Lenny sipped his Coke and looked out the window at the evening traffic and pretended he wasn't listening.

"The kid's polite and all. Has a super jump shot. His academics—I'm skeptical. If he ever took the SATs or that other test, his scores are a secret."

"Cliff, the college used to have standards."

"How many graduates become doctors or judges or senators or whatever doesn't excite alumni giving like athletic success does. Fields of glory, as some writer put it."

"Then Mr. Wallace is a field hand."

"I believe the writer had football in mind, but, yes, you're right. Wallace Wallace is here to help Bliss's boys win games, get to postseason, which translates into publicity, which opens pocketbooks and improves the flow of perpetually needed funds."

"Cliff, we've been down this road before. Let Division I schools go dark and soil themselves with athletics. Prester doesn't need it."

The student replaced the magazine he'd been scanning in the rack with the others. Avoiding eye contact, he started toward the door. "Titwit," Red remarked. The student nodded sheepishly and kept going. The bell tinkled as he closed the door.

"Okay," Red continued, "the girl—what's her name, your neighbor?"

"Maisie."

"You fixed her up with a press pass. I've seen her go by with Mr. Wallace, not exactly holding hands, but sort of rubbing up against him. Rubbed me the wrong way."

"She's Professor Thorne's daughter. Has a bit of a reputation."

"What's she need a press pass for?"

"To contemplate the form and grace of the male body in motion—Mr. Wallace's in particular. He's impressive."

"You suppose she wants to do more than observe?"

"Be my guess. What's yours?"

"Bragging rights. I got the star of the basketball team in the palm of my hand."

"In the sheets is more like it."

"You sure?"

"I hear people in the hall. I know when she has company and how long they stay."

"I've seen the Black girl from the drugstore walking with him."

"Mr. Wallace better be careful. He might fatigue himself and not play up to his potential."

"Oh, to be eighteen again."

"Wallace is nineteen. He dropped out of school twice to work and help support his family."

"Doesn't make him special. Plenty of white kids do the same thing."

"True enough, but they don't have Wallace's skills and his potential. They drop out and stay out."

"And do something useful, like laying brick or nailing up houses."

⁂

No car but there was Maisie slumped on the trailer steps. She wore a purple T-shirt under her denim jacket. Lenny pulled her up and brushed off mud dried on her jeans.

She wasn't sure if the boy's name was Bob or Bill. They met at the lake, drank, did other stuff. He took off. She drank some more. Driving home, she clipped a mailbox, overcorrected, swerved into a yard, skidded across the lawn, and crashed into a garage. A man pulled her out of her car. She promised to pay the damages. He kept her license and keys. She started walking. She didn't remember the man's name.

"How much?" Lenny asked.

"Five hundred for the lawn and garage."

"What about the car?"

"Shit. I don't know. Five hundred more?"

"Have it?"

"No."

"Borrow from mom?"

She shook her head. When Lenny let her out on College Street, she said, "I have friends in high places."

Later he realized that Cliff Barrow was probably looking down at them from his window.

⁂

Warner coughed and crossed his arms. He leaned against the sink and watched Lenny finish his Wheaties. "If you drive over to Mr. Peterson's property, you'll see where a couple of days ago Miss Maisie decided to take a shortcut across his yard.

Unfortunately, a garage got in her way. No one hurt, though I expect Miss Maisie's pocketbook will suffer some bruises."

"What about her Bug?"

"That's where she was lucky. Lots of front-end damage, but not enough impact for the gas tank to rupture like it does on those cars sometimes. Going to cost some bucks to make the car right again. I should have warned her."

"About drinking and driving?"

"About not having a Bower sticker on her car. Her mother's Skylark has one, but the Bug doesn't. If I had enforced the rules, she wouldn't have been on the property messing with whoever and wouldn't have done what she did."

"She would have found a way," Lenny said, then paused. "You said you wanted a favor."

"The day after the accident Miss Maisie showed up with enough cash to repair the lawn and the garage. Peterson agreed not to file any insurance claims or say anything to the village constabulary, though I suspect they know about it. Apparently, Maisie's parents do not, and Maisie wants to keep it that way. Peterson is a retired Delta pilot. He's treating the incident as a learning experience. He's willing to let Maisie call the shots, take responsibility. She'd like to have her car towed here and left, covered with a tarp, until she can get an estimate about the bodywork."

"Okay with me. Leave it around back, out of sight."

Lenny carried his bowl and glass to the sink. "Almost forgot," Warner said, "Mr. Harrison asked me to ask you if you could stop by late today. Be a lot easier, Lenny, if you had a phone instead of people calling me to contact you."

Another morning in the library. Noon, the lunch counter

was crowded. Vickie didn't have much time to talk. Wallace stopped by Lenny's cubicle before practice. He was nearly finished with the book. Maisie said he depended on Lenny too much. He wanted to try and write the report himself. Lenny asked if she was helping him. No, you're my man, he said. He promised to show Lenny the report before he turned it in.

ZEPHYR WORE A T-SHIRT AND cotton trousers gathered at the waist by the drawstring. He pointed to the painting leaning against the wall in the corner of the studio. She was naked, the young woman in the foreground, who stood on the shore in sunlight and gazed at her reflection rippling and hazy on the mirror of water that extended to the horizon.

"Haley," Zephyr said. "She paid. I painted her the way she wanted." He pointed to the surface. "Monet-ish, quick brushstrokes, not really my style. She was lovely—sensual and spiritual. I tried to paint her confusions, the way she saw herself. Bright bits and pieces. Nearly my worst effort, one huge cliché, but she liked it. She paid. She owns it. I keep it in case she ever comes back and wants it."

"You think that's going to happen?"

"I await our Savior's coming in glory, so why not?" He handed Lenny an envelope. "Snapshots Miss M took."

Four three-by-five prints. Lenny laid them on the table: long shot of Haley and Zephyr on the shore, looking off at the water; medium distance, Zephyr setting up his easel, Haley at the edge of the frame, looking back at the camera, frowning perhaps, difficult to interpret; Haley undressed, one foot in the water; Haley dressed in a riding outfit, standing in front of the Harrisons' house.

"She liked horses," Zephyr said, so softly he might have been whispering to himself.

Home again. Maisie's Bug was behind the trailer. Lenny lifted the tarp. A new quarter panel and hood would be needed. Two tires and front-end work. The windshield was cracked. An empty Gordon's vodka bottle lay in the passenger's seat. The window was down.

Lenny reached through and opened the glovebox. Lipsticks, tampons, cigarettes, and a three-pack of condoms with one left.

THE BASKETBALL ARENA SEATED eleven hundred. Lenny had never seen it full before. He inched into a seat at the end of the small faculty-staff section. Five cheerleaders—two men, three women—pranced onto the court, one man pushing a ceremonial broom as if vanquishing debris (how many colleges had an inanimate mascot?), the invisible opposition. The crowd cheered. The visiting team appeared. The crowd booed. The Sweepers appeared. The crowd rose and clapped.

Wallace Wallace scored thirty-five points before Bliss took him out with Prester ahead by twenty-five. Eight years since the school had won an opening game. Leaving the gym, Lenny saw Nathan Bullard, the college's president, with Wade DeFoe and another man, whom he recognized as a local judge and head of the board of trustees. A reporter from the *View* was trying to interview them.

Sandy had secured Lenny a permit to park behind the gym by the loading dock. The overhead doors were open. A truck for the crew breaking down the concession stand.

Vickie was sitting on his Jeep. "You don't look pleased to see me," she said. She tucked a roll of lifesavers into the pocket of the smock she was wearing.

"Surprised is more like it."

She pointed to the trees beyond the curve of cars belonging to coaches and staff. "Good place to be alone or with someone you want to be alone with."

"Like Wallace?" Lenny asked.

"He got plans tonight, snuggling with his white girl—Crazy Maisie."

"Is she?"

"He's crazy for her."

"Are you crazy for him?"

"He's an improvement over Carleton."

Lenny had an opinion on the subject but didn't say it. "How did you know my car was here?"

"I work concession. When we were setting up, I saw it."

"You want a ride?"

"Depends," she said. "You ever kiss a Black girl?"

"No."

"You want to do it here, or do you want to traipse into the trees?"

"I'm too tired for traipsing."

Vickie twisted off her seat and eased down from the car. Her tongue was languid, her mouth minty. She stepped away and wiped Lenny's lips with the sleeve of her shirt. "I'd like that ride you mentioned."

The nights were cold now, and the Jeep's heater didn't work. Vickie shivered. Passing the drugstore, she pointed up at the window of Maisie's apartment. "Wallace spends lots of time there," she said. "Hope he don't bust something."

"Hope he's working on his book report."

"Nah, he already turned it in."

"You sure?"

"He bragged he was going to get an A, and you'd be real proud of him."

❧

THE ENGLISH DEPARTMENT WAS ON the second floor of Hayes Hall across Old Quad from Mori. At nine the next morning, Lenny was waiting at Professor Fleck's office door. Ten minutes later he appeared, briefcase in hand, a tweed topcoat caped his shoulders, his bowtie slightly askew. He frowned at Lenny and searched his jacket pocket for his key. "I can't recall your name."

"Leonard Grey."

"Of course. You won the department's essay prize, didn't you?"

"Twice."

"Years ago was it?"

"Second time was last year."

"Seems longer ago than that, but at my age one's sense of chronology becomes skewed."

Fleck opened the door. Lenny inhaled the suffocating scent of the lilies in the pot on a table by the bookcase. A large conch shell weighed down a pile of student papers on the edge of Fleck's desk. "Work that *shell* be done." He chuckled and shrugged off his coat.

"I tutor one of your students," Lenny said. "Mr. Wallace."

"Ah, yes, the repetitive Mr. Wallace. Or WW as his confreres call him. Win-win." Fleck pointed to the papers. "I haven't gotten around to any of these yet, but I was pleasantly surprised to notice he typed his or someone did. His handwriting is atrocious."

Fleck sorted through the papers. "Here's your man." He pulled out two pages, neatly typed and stapled together: **A Book Report on Mr. Hemingway's The Old Man and the Sea by Wallace Wallace.** "Might have italicized Hemingway's title, but...we shall see, won't we." Fleck returned Wallace's report to the pile. "What's on your mind, Mr. Grey?"

"I'd like to look over Mr. Wallace's paper."

"Surely, you must have already seen it."

"I haven't. Not the final version."

Fleck shrugged. "I'm not sure what difference seeing it will make now."

"Professional responsibility."

Fleck retrieved Wallace's report and handed it to Lenny. "Return it by noon."

Lenny walked and read. "In this gem of short fiction, the master is at it again. Add Santiago to the long list of Hemingway heroes. Know them by the purity and simplicity of their courage, their grace under pressure, their..." Lenny remembered reading those words in an essay on Hemingway's late fiction, but he couldn't recall who wrote them. Certainly not Wallace.

Plagiarism. No denying it. Lenny clutched the report in one hand and took deep breaths. Surprise, disappointment, anger—he tried to calm himself and focus on Wallace, but

Maisie kept getting in the way. Maisie and who else? Lenny believed in Wallace's honesty. He wouldn't throw it away.

Sandy's office door slammed open. She was on the phone. "I'll call you back," she said and hung up. "Lenny—"

"I need a desk and a typewriter."

"Don't shout."

"Right now."

She picked up the report that he had slapped down in front of her, skimmed the first paragraph, hunched over her desk, and sighed. "What should we do?"

"Write the report Wallace might have written."

"Lenny, you sure?"

"I remember the book well enough."

"That's not what I'm asking."

"Don't say it. I know the rules."

"Lenny, be sensible. You have Wallace's paper in hand. Keep it. Talk to Wallace, explain the problem, ask Fleck for an extension, give Wallace another chance to complete the assignment on his own."

"Fleck hasn't read what Wallace turned in. He'll believe what I turn in."

"Lenny, I don't understand."

"This isn't Wallace's fault."

"It's his mistake."

"I let him go off on his own. It's mine."

"You can't unmake it."

"I can try."

Sandy led him to an empty desk in another office. "Typed on a Selectric. It's what we use. We can match the font. This person's away. Take your time."

An hour later Lenny placed one typed page, stapled to the original cover page, on top of the other reports on Fleck's desk. He said, "I understand Mr. Wallace recently put on a show."

"He's something," Lenny said, but plagiarist, he thought, was not one of them.

❧

THE NEXT DAY LENNY BOUGHT a copy of the View to read in his cubicle while he waited for the giggly tennis players. "Dark Days Ahead" was the title of "Cliff's Notes." He wrote about golden autumn fading into winter's gloom, how once upon a time seasonal darkness relieved only by the thin flame of a candle provided opportunity for contemplation and ruminating on the baffling questions of mortality. Now, however, the incandescent bulb allowed an artificial lightenment that did not lead as much to enlightenment as excitement and spectacle, which (the writer realized how unpopular it was to express it) included sports that regrettably required an ever larger serving of Prester's budget—which was never as nourishing as needed to grow and maintain the health of the arts and sciences that sustained mind and imagination, *mens* and *imaginatio*, the words that appeared on the great seal of the college and honored the heritage of Caedmon Prester, who brought the light of learning to a dark wilderness.

Professor Fleck materialized, somewhat breathless, in the doorway. "Ah, is this your lair then." Lenny pushed a chair in Fleck's direction. "No need. I shall not tarry." From his topcoat pocket he withdrew Wallace's report and tossed it onto the table. "Most amusing."

"Amusing?"

"Mr. Grey, if you had been sitting in an office like mine and someone slid a large envelope under your door, what would you assume?"

"One of my students was handing in his assignment."

"Which I did. I am surprisingly agile and quick when I need to be. I leapt from my chair, flung open the door, and glimpsed a coed with a shapely derriere disappearing down the hall—Miss Thorne, I believe. I have had occasion to observe her and Mr. Wallace striding across campus together. How thoughtful of her to deliver Mr. Wallace's report a bit before it was due." Fleck regarded the chair. "Perhaps I will sit down," he said.

He crossed his legs and draped his topcoat over his knees. "I fibbed when I told you I had not read Mr. Wallace's submission, which you took away and discovered what we both know is not his work."

Lenny retreated to the other side of the table. Fleck continued, "What to think, what to do?" He stared up at the stained ceiling panels, then back at Lenny. "The work is obviously a violation of Prester's honor code, but how responsible is Wallace? Does he possess the research skills to find a relevant essay on Hemingway's work? Yes, probably, with the help of a librarian. Does he possess the editorial skill to take from it and shape it into a slender book report? Probably not. For the moment let's put aside the question whether you would or did the editing and shaping. Would Wallace be foolish enough to think he could plagiarize and get away with it? I'm not sure, but I lean toward no. You, however, had no qualms about writing a report he could pass off as his own."

"I talked myself into it."

"Why? I can scarcely believe you were in Mr. Wallace's debt. You might, as the Brits say, be sent down for violating the college's honor code."

"It's possible."

"What were you going to say to Mr. Wallace?"

"I had gotten him out of one mess and wouldn't do it again."

"But why even once?"

"I don't want him sent down."

"*Sent back* is more like it, back to the piney woods, back to obscurity and scraping by."

"That's my point."

Fleck picked at a thread on his topcoat. "If Wallace did plan to submit someone else's work, he did not actually do it. Miss Thorne did. Whatever he may have intended—and I'm not a mind reader—technically Wallace didn't cheat. He did not, in the words of the rulebook, 'submit another's work as his own.'"

"He doesn't know I wrote a report for him either."

"Mr. Grey, trust me. If Mr. Wallace or his associates submitted any work in his name, I did not receive it and have no knowledge of such a thing happening. Furthermore," Fleck stood up, "if I possessed such knowledge, I would keep it to myself. Mr. Wallace may have extra time to complete the assignment. Tell him I lost his first effort." Fleck put on his coat. "See you at teatime."

Lenny had forgotten about the tea, an event the English department hosted every autumn. The department faculty socialized with its undergraduate majors, drinking tepid Tetley, nibbling bland cookies, exchanging uncomfortable small talk.

The event was held in a reception room in Thebes Hall, the main campus dining facility. Lenny snuck in by a side door to avoid the receiving line. Professor Crane, whose novel course he was enrolled in, spotted him, dressed in his dead man's clothes, lingering near two potted palms. Lenny and Crane chatted about the books he had assigned and passed on one piece of department news: Oswald Fleck, though close to retirement, was going to be named Distinguished Professor of Rhetoric, an honor that came with a handsome financial benefit. The idea—a scandal, really—was President Bullard's. Most of Fleck's department were in shock and disbelief.

Five o'clock, Sandy stopped Lenny on Old Quad. Twenty minutes later they ordered drinks at the Cat.

"You and Fleck…what's up?"

"He's being honored."

"By his department? Sounds improbable."

"By Bullard. Fleck is now the college's Distinguished Professor of Rhetoric."

"You suspect something isn't kosher?"

"College politics are out of my league."

"Let's get specific. You exchanged a paper an athlete didn't write for one you wrote and handed it in for him." Sandy downed her drink and signaled for another. "Lenny, you're going to need an ally. Besides me, who else have you got?"

"Bliss?"

"Perhaps."

The server dressed in impossibly tight leggings winked at Lenny as she passed behind the bar. "She had her eye on you the first time we were here. If I were her age, I'd do the same thing. You seeing anyone?"

"Vickie from the drugstore kissed me. That's about it."

"When I was your age, a white student kissing a Black

townie didn't happen unless money was involved. None was, I assume."

"One kiss, no charge."

Sandy's fresh drink arrived. She raised the glass, thought a minute, then put it down. "I give Bliss credit for recruiting Black players, though I understand full well his motive is winning games not changing society or Prester's culture. I doubt he cares about that one way or another. Were there any Black people where you grew up?"

"I never saw one."

"I was raised two counties east of here. Back then the Klan was big. They don't dress up, march around, and burn crosses anymore, but their hearts and minds haven't changed. Prester was always the liberal community, but the school didn't admit more than the token Black. Even now there's only a few. A few too many some people think—Cliff Barrow for one."

Sandy didn't put her glass down this time. She finished her drink and gazed into the distance. Finally, she focused on Lenny again. "Let's get this straight—Fleck has read two book reports with Wallace Wallace's name on them, the one Maisie delivered and the one you replaced it with."

"Correct."

"Fleck could make trouble for Wallace—and you, especially you—but he won't. He's protecting Wallace. In your own way, you did the same thing, but you weren't using him. Understand?"

"Bullard and Fleck are working together."

"*Plotting* is more like it. Fleck leveraged the plagiarized report to help himself. Bliss doesn't get to recruit unqualified players without Bullard's approval. Both men need a winning season—Bliss for himself and his own career, Bullard to create publicity and pump up alumni giving, which has been short of expectations lately."

Sandy took a deep breath. "Okay. Fleck shows Bullard a plagiarized report with Wallace's name on it, which opens the way for Bullard and Fleck to join up for their mutual benefit. Of course, someone other than Wallace has to hand in the report, thereby putting the kibosh on any charge of an honor code violation, which would lead to Wallace's expulsion, and, clearly, that is not the intended result. All very neat on the surface, very murky underneath."

Sandy spun her empty glass, watching how it refracted the light above the bar. "Did Wallace ever write anything? Did someone volunteer to help him out and write a report for him and turn it in? Would Wallace let that happen? Everything depends on it happening, but how did it happen? Who *did* write the report?"

Sandy reached into her handbag for her wallet. "How did you find out Wallace had gone off on his own and completed the assignment without your help?"

"Wallace told me that Maisie encouraged him to write the report himself. She said he depended on me too much."

"But he didn't write it. Who did? Maisie?"

"A long shot."

"However, she *did* hand it in." Sandy paid the check. They stood in the parking lot. The sky was clouding over. More rain was forecast, followed by the first frost.

"Cliff Barrow," Lenny said.

The floodlight on the pole in the yard shone on Lia's car parked in front of the trailer. She got out and stepped on the cigarette she'd been smoking. "I would've waited inside, but I didn't want to discover any secrets."

Lenny slammed the Jeep's door shut. "Like what?"

"Nothing specific, but we all have secrets. Tell me, is Maisie providing compensation for guarding her car, keeping it out of sight? I'm here to check on its condition."

"Did she tell you what happened?"

"Of course not. We hardly see each other and don't say much when we do. I prefer we continue the illusion I suspect nothing."

"How did you find out?"

"I prefer not to say."

"If you've seen the damage, now what?"

"Lenny, you're a bit sharp tonight. Ease up. You put the motor in shape. I assume you don't do body work. I'm referring to motor vehicles."

"Maisie plans to have a shop in Graham fix the car when she can pay the bill."

"No services were promised or exchanged for storing the car on your lawn?"

"Don't need any."

Lia wore a cable-knit sweater and an old pair of bellbottoms. She said, "I'm cold. Can we finish our conversation in your trailer or my car?"

"My heat isn't on."

She laughed. "I assume you're referring to the trailer."

Seated in the car again, Lenny beside her, she started the motor and turned the heater to max. "Any idea where Maisie is going to get money for repairs?"

"She didn't say."

"I hear tutoring pays well."

"Not enough for me to help Maisie."

"But enough for you?"

"Depends on how many hours I put in."

"You spend much time writing papers for the basketball guy?"

"His name is Wallace. He writes his own—I help him."

"Thomas says the league has a most valuable player award. He thinks there should be one for the most valuable tutor."

"Does he go to the games?"

"He's attended the two so far. Your Mr. Wallace scored thirty-five in one and thirty-eight in the other. Very impressive." Lia tilted her seat and leaned back. Her sweater was coming apart. The light was enough for Lenny to see part of her breast. "Thomas isn't the only faculty member with questions about the tutoring program."

"I only know what I do with the athletes I'm assigned."

"I wish you'd take Maisie under your wing. She seems determined to star in the same anemic academic performance she gave in Colorado."

"I'm sure she's good at other things."

"Driving isn't one of them. Any advice?"

"She might like a theater course that includes reading and acting."

"She seems to be creating her own little dramas. There's you, there's the Bower boy—or boys—and who knows who else."

"Mr. Wallace."

"Really? Shows how open minded she is. Then there's Cliff Barrow—if you can believe that. Know him?"

"Not well."

"Me either. We had a fling once. He's beer, I'm whiskey—single malt. He's rough and tumble, I'm slow and deep."

"It's late," Lenny said.

Lia reached over and curved her fingers around his. "I haven't been touched by a man since the night you waited on Thomas and me at the Nook." She slid Lenny's hand under her sweater and sighed. "I could tell you lots of stories about being with boys in cars." Her skin felt cold where Lenny touched her. "But I'm not sure you're in the mood to hear them."

Dobo's daughter lived with her mother in another town. She was twelve and pretty and knew it. She tie-dyed shirts and made candles, which she sold on the street. Her mother worried about the men who offered her money but not for shirts or candles. I convinced Dobo to let his daughter have a space in the lobby of the Azul and sell her work there. Most days she never showed up, and I would keep watch for customers. Other people began to bring belts and blankets and sandals they'd made, better to display them inside the cool lobby than outside under the sultry shade of a drooping canvas, which collapsed in the afternoon rains. Safer too. There were always thieves about. I tended the merchandise and charged a commission. Without intending to, I became a capitalist in a system I had run away from. At least I was helping the artisans of the local economy. I didn't know what to make of it or myself. Then I got the idea of renting a shed that

once had been a stable and setting up booths where people who made things could sell them. I charged just enough to pay rent to the owner. Dobo didn't like the idea because it diminished the number of tourists that often crowded the hotel lobby and lingered in the bar on rainy afternoons. But the sellers liked it, and when they called me La Gringa, *they spoke with respect. I moved into a room on the third floor and settled into a new life.*

I met Marco, and we became lovers. He had gone to the university and studied law. His job in Guadalajara didn't start for another month. He was idling away the time on the beach or at the bar before leaving. He seemed ambivalent about a legal career. For the moment I was his passion—me and photography. He corresponded with several photographers. The only one I'd heard of was Alvarez Bravo because Dobo admired him, too, and owned a book of his photographs. The pages of nudes were well thumbed.

One day Marco drove us to an abandoned hacienda and took pictures of me waving my shirt like a cape before an imaginary bull in a dusty ring surrounded by a low wall of crumbing bricks. We saw fresh footprints in the sand and were sure we were being watched by vagrants and scavengers hiding behind the hacienda's empty windows. We left, Marco pulling me by the hand as I looked back, scanning the tilted balconies for a face. Perhaps by chance I had found the home of the dropouts and mellow riffraff I had planned to join, the few who might remain, but I saw no signs of the arbors and gardens we vowed to grow so we could sustain ourselves and help heal the planet.

IV

Wallace shuffled into the cubicle and unzipped his suede jacket, which looked new and expensive.

"Wallace, sorry there is a problem. Fleck's old and absent-minded. He probably mislaid your book report somewhere. Whatever the reason, he can't find it, so we need you to hand in another copy. Doesn't have to be typed."

"I kept my first draft. I reworked it some, tried to make my letters better, but the report I handed in and what you got in your hand, they mostly the same." He sat down and gave Lenny a handwritten page torn from a lined composition book.

The story is about fishing. An old guy named Santiago hasn't caught a fish in a long time. People think he's bad luck. They don't believe in him no longer except for Manolin, a young kid. The old guy hooks a big marlin and can't let go. The fish pulls the old guy around the ocean for three days. Then it gives up. The old guy kills the fish but sharks attack it because they smell blood. The old guy has to go home with bones left of the fish. It's bigger than any people had ever seen. Manolin and the old man stay friends.

"Fleck pass it, you think? Coach checked. All I need is a C minus."

"Before we talk about that, tell me who typed what you wrote."

"Miss Maisie said she knew someone who would do it. She'd carry it to her, then carry it to Dr. Fleck's office."

"Less than a page. Maisie could have typed it herself."

"She would have but she said hers was broken."

"Hers?"

"Her typewriter. She told me what kind it was. Royal, I think. You cross I did the writing on my own? and didn't show it to you?"

"No, but I think you can write something better."

"I did like Fleck asked. I reported what happened."

Lenny folded the page and laid it on the table. "Why do you think Hemingway wrote the story? Santiago, the old guy, what were his thoughts about the fish?"

"It was a fighter."

"Do you think you might include some of that, what was going through Santiago's mind?"

Wallace frowned. "Mr. Lenny, if you was a reporter and the boss told you to write a report about a holdup and you wrote where it happened and who it happened to and how much was taken and what the robber looked like and if anyone was caught or not, wouldn't that be doing what the boss asked? He didn't want stuff about what the victim was thinking."

"I get your point, but usually a book report includes more than an account of who did what with whom. Is Santiago heroic?"

"He fought the fish and the ocean, then the sharks came.

I've never seen the ocean, but I know it's mighty big. I never seen a shark either, but I know they mean."

"What about rattlesnakes?"

"I know them. They mean."

"Were you a hero when you picked up the one in the crib?"

"I did what I had to."

"Santiago's an old man. Was fishing something he had to do?"

"I have to think."

"Think more about the book. What is Hemingway telling us? What can we learn from an old man's struggle with a huge fish in a huge ocean?"

"You're saying if Fleck was the boss, he'd want me to write about the victim afraid the gun would go off and he would wet his pants?"

"Something like that," Lenny said.

Wallace stood and pushed the page into his pocket. "Anything else?"

"How is Maisie?"

"Not seen her much. She said she had lots of work to do."

Lenny admired Wallace's jacket. "Mr. DeFoe, he saw me in my raggedy flannel one and told me to stop at that store on Hawthorne Street and pick out something warmer and put it on his account."

Lenny and Wallace walked down the hallway to the door to the parking lot. "It's so different here," he said. "Like in the store. All those expensive clothes and me feeling I was trespassing and the clerk giving me the eye like I was right. Back home everyone is the same. Everyone is poor. White or Black, no matter. Everyone talks to each other because we be the same. There is never a place for whites where I can't go. Like the preacher say, we born poor, we die poor, and in between we share our daily bread."

The team bus from the school Prester was playing that night was parked near the loading dock. The sky was gray. "Ever snow here?" Wallace asked.

"Some, but not much."

"Next week Thanksgiving. I'd like to visit home, but the team traveling to Wilmington."

"You'll see the ocean."

"Rather see home. My uncle always sneak a bird from the poultry plant where he works, usually a fat turkey, and my aunt cooks up a feast. What about you?"

"Beans and rice."

"By yourself?"

"Probably."

"I hear Miss Maisie wrecked her vehicle and it's where you live. There's a wild streak in her. You ever been to her house?"

"Last summer. I did some work for her mother."

"She drove me over there once, but I stayed in the car, didn't get out."

"Were you invited to?"

"I can't say for sure. Miss Maisie said I could come in if I wanted."

"But you didn't?"

"She didn't sound encouraging."

"Since you've been here, has anyone told you not to come in or to leave?"

"No, but I get a lot of unfriendly looks, like the one the clerk gave me when I pointed to the jacket. It pained him to take if off the hanger. He laid it on the counter, wouldn't hand it to me."

"How did Mr. Barrow treat you when he interviewed you?"

"Polite. He asked about my family and my coaches, what kind of facilities my school had, stuff like that. I thought he'd take my picture, but he didn't."

"Keep playing the way you've been, and the paper will print lots of pictures of you."

Wallace laughed. "I send copies home, so my momma don't forget my face."

❧

AUTUMN WAS THINNING INTO WINTER. Days in the sixties, frosty nights. Lenny ran on the indoor track and showered in the gym. The *View* published a recap of the Prester-Wilmington game under the headline Sweepers Stun Seahawks. First time Prester had defeated a Division I school since the baseball team beat Chapel Hill in 1913. Wallace scored forty-one.

Lenny spent the holiday break writing an essay on Edith Wharton. Growing up in Maine, he had heard people remember what their parents said about seeing Miss Wharton when she visited a friend's estate near Bar Harbor. She was aloof and elegant. Erskine Caldwell's brief appearance one more recent summer was recalled differently. He drove a Cadillac, undoubtedly paid for by the royalties from the trashy books he wrote about trashy people. He wore expensive shoes and no socks. The woman with him probably wasn't his wife.

When Lenny decided to attend Prester and not Dartmouth, his mother said it wasn't the climate that persuaded him as much as putting as many miles between her and him as possible. Most nights she slept over with the man she'd been seeing before Lenny's father drowned, his toolbox lashed to his leg. Wasn't suicide, the coroner said. Your dad got tangled up and fell overboard. Happens more often than you think.

After a string of dull days, a bright Indian-summer afternoon. It was time to put the solar shower away for another year. Seventy degrees, Lenny guessed. Warm enough. He took off his shirt, pushed down his jeans, and stepped out of them. The plastic water bag he always refilled after he used it was empty. He wondered if the McGoon sisters had resumed playing tricks.

"If you're doing something kinky with that shower thing, keep on. I'll just watch." Maisie cocked her hip, twirled her sunglasses, and waited for an answer.

"Cleaning up," Lenny mumbled and reached for his clothes.

"Stay like you are. I stopped to ask if you wanted to lie out at the lake with me, but I'll get naked and we can do it here. Nobody can see us from the road."

"You have a car?"

She flapped her arms. "No, I grew wings."

"I meant, whose car?"

"My neighbor's." She continued to stare and smile and twirl her sunglasses. Lenny continued to stand and be stared at. "What's it going to be?"

"Give me a minute. I'll drive to the lake."

She said, "I'll check out the Bug."

He dressed and retrieved the Jeep's key from the trailer. Maisie had pulled off the tarp. She pointed to the crumpled cellophane wrapper on the floormat. "Somebody's been sitting in here snacking." She bent down. "Seats have been pushed back, like the person wanted to stretch out and sleep. I tried that a couple of times. Wasn't to sleep, though."

"How long do you plan to leave the car here?"

"I'm still making financial arrangements."

"No hurry," he said.

"Good," Maisie said. "Gives me an excuse to stop by and see you." She chuckled. "Saw a lot today, more than I expected."

Lenny noticed the Bower sticker on the Dodge Maisie had borrowed. "Whose car? Cliff Barrow's?"

"So what?"

"What do you do for him?"

"Not as much as I'm willing to do for you. What do you have in mind?"

"You encouraged Wallace Wallace to write his book report without my help, then you handed in one he didn't write."

"The first part, yes. The second never happened."

"An envelope slides under Professor Fleck's door. He sees you disappearing down the hall."

Maisie was no longer amused. She looked Lenny up and down, then stepped closer and fixed her attention on his face. "Aren't you falling for one of those logic things with impossible Latin names—because of this, therefore that, or something? Other people were in the hall."

"You know because you were there?"

Maisie squeezed her lips into a tense smile. "English is a popular major. People are always in the hall."

"You signed up for West's Victorian fiction course. How's that going?"

"I dropped it weeks ago. My eyes couldn't take all that reading."

"Then why were you hanging around the department offices?"

"Okay, I wasn't hanging around. Cliff's a neighbor. He asked me to deliver an envelope to Fleck's office. He didn't say what was in it."

"Now you know."

"No, I don't. I did Cliff a favor is what I know. The contents of the envelope could be anything."

"They just happened to be sentences from an essay about the book Wallace was supposed to write a report on."

"He cheated, you mean? Plagiarized, or whatever?"

"Yes."

"Was it typed?"

"Yes."

"Wallace doesn't type."

"You would know that because he gave you what he wrote to have it typed."

"Yes and no. What he gave me was in an envelope—"

"One page and an envelope was required and he happened to have one?"

"I brought it with me because eventually I knew I would need it."

"Or Cliff would."

"Jesus, Lenny, you've found me out. Where envelopes are concerned, I can't tell one from another. The one with the report Wallace handed me and the one Cliff gave me to give Fleck looked the same—tan color with a clasp shaped like an insect with wings on the flap."

"Do you type?"

Maisie wiggled her fingers. "My touch is exquisite. Typing

is only one of their talents. I can demonstrate."

"You could have typed Wallace's report."

"I could have. I didn't because I have enough work of my own to type and typing isn't a favor I do for other people. Didn't want any hurt feelings, so I told Wallace my Royal was broken. I took his report in the envelope to a woman who works at the *View*. Typing student papers is a side business of hers. She has a reputation for correcting grammar and finding typos, sort of like you. I assumed whatever Wallace wrote would need her skills. For damn sure I don't have them."

"What's the woman's name?"

"She prefers to remain anonymous. *View* employees aren't allowed to use office equipment for outside jobs."

Lenny glared at Maisie. She glared at him. "Listen up—I never opened any envelope. I never saw what was inside any envelope, and you can't prove I did. No way. Furthermore, if anyone tells you you're cute when you're angry, you're not."

❧

PALE SKY. NO BIRDS, not even pigeons. Welcome to winter. The library was closed. Lenny dropped the books he'd borrowed into the return chute and trudged across campus, enjoying the solitude. Sandy waved from her office window. She put on a jacket and caught up with him. "It's Sunday. Can't you stay away?"

"Can't you?"

"Too much work," she said. "I'm trying to get ahead of the end-of-term rush."

"Cliff Barrow—give me a history lesson."

"His maternal line is from the Spiveys—hill people—who farmed as best they could on land where the Bower is now. They had a reputation for stilling decent whiskey.

"Barrow's father's people raised and butchered hogs. The parcel of land where the college junks worn-out furniture and equipment was once part of Cliff's great-grandfather's farm. The college acquired it from Cliff's grandfather, who kept enough to continue the family tradition of producing tasty pork much admired throughout the area.

"As the college expanded, the Barrows sold it most of their acreage. Athletic fields occupy some of it now. Cliff's father continued to keep pigs on what was left until the school made him a lucrative offer that included a provision that allowed Cliff, who was only a year old then, to attend the college free of charge, which eventually he did.

"He presented himself as a tobacco-chewing townie. He dressed in work shirts, overalls, and boots, nothing like the clothes in the fancy shops on Hawthorne Street. He wasn't social. No dates or dances or frat parties. He lived off campus. His classmates considered him a rough cob, but most of his professors saw him as a rough diamond. He majored in English and minored in classical languages."

"Sounds as if he was."

"And proud of it. There was an unfortunate incident in a Latin class. The professor, an older gentleman, asked Cliff to stand and translate a poem of Catullus. When Cliff finished, the professor praised him, saying the translation was particularly skillful when spoken by the son of a pig farmer. Cliff was stung. Instead of sitting down, he asked how the professor's father had made a living. A surgeon, the professor replied. To which Cliff said that both their families had blood on their hands.

"The professor canceled class. Cliff was summoned to the president's office and lectured on respect and academic deportment. Cliff wrote an essay on academic snobbery that the *Sweeper* would have published had not the dean stopped it and threatened to expel Cliff, the free-tuition arrangement notwithstanding."

Sandy and Lenny kept walking. "Publicly, the college pretends to admire Cliff—a son of the soil, graduated with honors, served his country in Vietnam. Privately, Bullard loathes him. A royal pain in the ass, always finding fault with how the school raises money and how it spends it. Dolts with dough are welcome. Children of pig farmers are not.

"Cliff's always been critical of how much Prester spends to promote itself as a bucolic, nourishing environment, a healthy place for mind and body. Of course, young people drink too much, experiment with drugs—the minor ones—and have sex, but it's better done here amid the hallowed halls and rustic safety of a caring college with a distinguished faculty than in the real world."

"Now he's onto athletics," Lenny said.

"If what you suspect happened and he's responsible for the book report Wallace didn't write, he's *into* athletics. He's not standing on the sidelines. I hope you don't get punished for your part in what happened."

"Only Barrow, Bullard, and Fleck know what happened. I don't think they're going public."

"You know."

"Not everything. If Cliff substituted a plagiarized report for the one Wallace wrote and expected Fleck to turn Wallace in for cheating and have him expelled, it didn't work. Instead, Bullard and Fleck got what they wanted. Wallace is still playing."

"Lenny, what's your point?"

"There's trouble ahead."

"Lenny, the term's almost over. Think positive. Do you go anywhere at Christmas? Visit your mother?"

"She lives with a man in Vermont. They're not big on visitors."

"I always have a holiday party. You're invited."

"Need to tell you something," Warner said. He stepped inside the trailer. "Dawn the other morning, Smith was patrolling and thought he saw a person duck behind this place. By the time he parked and investigated, whoever it was had disappeared into the trees up the hillside."

"Before the weather changed, the person might have used my shower."

"Lenny, I realize you're very accommodating—fixing peoples' cars, letting them park here. I'm not sure what else, but you should buy a new lock, and exercise caution."

"The lock is on my chore list."

Warner coughed. "If you need extra cash, the Residents' Association will pay you to sub for me a couple of weeks in December, maybe longer, unless you've got plans yourself."

"No plans."

Lenny followed Warner outside and watched him squeeze

himself into his truck. “Got to slim down,” he said.

“Did Cliff Barrow ever live on the lake?”

“Not that I’m aware of.”

“His car has a Bower sticker.”

“The residents used to ask for extras to give to their friends so they could fish or swim in the lake, but then I heard lots of complaints, so I don’t give stickers out anymore, except to people like you who are on my team, so to speak. Not sure who Barrow might know. Some for sure don’t care for him—Wade DeFoe, for example. Could be Barrow has a sticker because some of the old families like his have kin buried on land that was acquired to create the lake and house sites. When the project was announced, people fussed about digging up bodies to make a swimming hole. All sorts of experts with special equipment mapped the area. In the end, the graves were located on the edge of the project where no excavation was planned. The dead were left to their peace. Whoever gave Barrow a sticker didn’t tell me about it, but you’re right, he has one.”

“You said Mr. DeFoe doesn’t care for Barrow.”

“DeFoe is all good news about the college. Read some of the stuff Barrow writes and you know he isn’t. Like last week he editorialized about the poor maintenance of the library—leaks, restroom graffiti, mold—and the spotless training rooms in the gym, the new exercise equipment, and the cost of refinishing the basketball floor every year. Apples to oranges in my opinion.

“Also, he’s pissed that the school rented two buses to deliver the basketball team to a Christmas tournament in Charleston—one for the players, coaches, and trainers, the other for alumni, donors, a bar, and a box of fancy souvenir brooms.”

⁂

Monday, Professor Hilton met Lenny on the way to his cubicle. "I've been reading faculty reports about your tutees—all positive. I commend you for a first-class job. Even Mr. Wallace is scraping by. Those Asian gals are pulling A's in chemistry and math. Good attitudes too. Your soccer player is a bit sarcastic, but his C's are about as much as we can expect of him, top of his academic game." Hilton squeezed Lenny's biceps, suggested he do some weight training, and headed in the opposite direction down the hall. Coach Bliss filled the doorway of the cubicle.

"You made Hilton a happy man," Bliss said. "Made the fans happy too. How about yourself—you happy?"

"I'm glad the term's about finished."

"Next one your last?"

"Might be."

"Then what?"

"A job." Lenny hoped Bliss wasn't about to offer a game plan for success based on basketball—the "front court of life," he had heard him refer to it.

"You don't sound happy," Bliss said.

"Lots on my mind."

"That Black girl I've seen you with, she on your mind?"

"We're friends."

"How close?"

"Not very."

"Prester's a special place. Protected, I mean. You can do things here that you can't somewhere else."

"Like have a Black girlfriend?"

"One thing I like about you, Lenny, I don't have to spell things out."

"She's not my girlfriend."

Bliss shrugged. "None of my concern, but as a person who has been around a bit, a white man with a Black girl is making trouble for himself—from both sides."

"Some trouble is worth it."

"Lenny, I don't disagree with you. Take Wallace, for example, Wallace and Tyrone. There's a bunch of locals who don't want them here, and I'd serve myself better by recruiting only white players, but I chose not to go that way, and Bullard and others have stood by me. Hell, it's been over a dozen years since Carolina put a Black player on the court and good things followed. We need to catch up."

Bliss paused to follow the progress of one of the secretaries tapping her way down the hall on spiky heels. "You ever been to Charleston?" he continued. "I can squeeze you onto the team bus for the Christmas tournament. You'd need to pay something for lodging, but I might could add you to the expense account, designate you as an assistant manager, or something."

"Coach, I appreciate the opportunity, but I promised someone I'd work for him over the holiday."

"Doing what?"

"Security at the lake."

"Carry a firearm?"

"No, sir."

"Ever shot a gun?"

"I have."

Bliss winked. "Good, because if you go out into the world with a Black girlfriend, you might have to do it again."

Sometimes I would spend the night at Marco's house: two rooms, cinderblock walls, and a flat roof—sheet metal from an abandoned factory laid over salvaged plywood. Grilles on the windows kept the monkeys out. Nothing deterred the scorpions.

There wasn't a door on the privy. As I hunched over the pit gouged out of the hard ground, monkeys would jump on my shoulders and play with my hair, which I would wash thoroughly and douse with a sulfurous chemical as soon as I returned to the Blue Hotel. You wouldn't have made a good hippie, Marco said.

He was right. It wasn't so much I wanted clean skin and clean sheets but that I liked making money and using my profits from the market to help families buy better food and pay for medicine. You a benevolent capitalist, Marco said.

Dobo warned me, and Marco agreed. You have money, he said. You from US, you pretty—you're being watched. Those fancy resorts along the beach, did I think men with two-way radios and automatic weapons patrolled the properties for exercise? Kidnapping was a major source of local income. Don't go back to the hacienda looking for the dropouts you hoped to find. Don't go anywhere alone.

I bought the .38 revolver from a retired federal officer who operated a pawnshop out of his house. He drove me in his Land Rover into the jungle where there were Mayan ruins in the dense cover of vines and leaves and taught me to load, aim, and shoot.

He asked me if I'd ever been attacked. I wasn't sure how much to tell him. I said once, when I was hitchhiking. Hacer dedo *was the phrase I wanted, but I didn't know it, and I mimed what I was talking about. He laughed and warned me not to thumb rides in Mexico. If I bought a car, I shouldn't drive it alone at night. If I wanted to buy a car, he could send me to people who would sell me a good one. I thought about my MG and wondered who owned it now. I'd given one set of keys to the man I sold it to and kept the other.*

V

None of Lenny's tutees showed up needing help. He had left the Jeep at the edge of the parking lot. Vickie was waiting for him, a towel on her lap, painting her fingernails. "This red too red?" she asked.

"Not for Christmas."

"Hadn't thought about that. Preacher Daddy won't like it."

"It's cheerful."

"Supposed to be sexy."

She capped the bottle and folded the towel. "Ride me somewhere."

Lenny chuckled and she frowned. "What's funny?"

"You want me to *drive* you somewhere."

"That's what I just said. You deaf?"

"Where is somewhere?"

"The lake. I bet lots of them houses are decorated real fine—trees and lights and all." She waved her hands in the air. "Dry enough," she said and leaned against Lenny's shoulder. She found his hand, raised it to her lips, sucked his finger. "Be dark soon," she said.

Her pants tapered to her ankles. She slid Lenny's hand over

her thigh. "I bought them at the place that sells old clothes—Vantage Shop."

"*Vintage.*"

"Right. What I got on was popular for skiing. Stirrup pants, the lady said. Going to be popular again." Vickie unzipped her jacket. "Doctor Teddy gave me this shirt last Christmas. Snug. He probably figured that. Shows me off. Smooth too. Want to feel?"

"I'll take your word for it."

"Fraidy cat." Vickie snickered and scrunched down in her seat. She didn't move until Lenny parked overlooking the lake.

They surveyed the houses across the water. "Disappointing," Vickie said. "Preacher Daddy already put up a tree with lights and angels and all, but these folks don't even have candles in the windows."

Lenny remembered the wreath on the door and the smell of Lysol inside the drab waiting room. On a sheet over a table, there was a plastic crèche with a pink Jesus. "Next week they will," he said.

"Trade places," she said. "No point in wasting an opportunity." She opened the door and got out. "Come on."

When Lenny was seated on the passenger's side, she raised herself up and settled on his lap, facing him, one leg stretched between the seats, the other between the seat and the door.

"You kiss good," she said. She unzipped her jacket again. The shirt did show her off. "You don't seem too enthusiastic. I'm not the wrong color, am I?"

"Not at all."

"You thought any about Wallace fooling with a white girl—Maisie?"

"He needs to be careful."

"Careful doing it, you mean?"

"No, she's using him for something. I don't know what."

"I do. She's telling herself he's got the goods to make her happy. That's what I hear a lot of white girls saying about Black men. They talk that stuff at the soda fountain right in front of me, like I'm not there."

"It's more than that."

Vickie found Lenny's hand again. "Cold out here. You going to warm me up?"

"You hungry?"

"What are you serving?"

"Pizza at my trailer."

She zipped up her jacket. "Is that as good as it gets? Then you ride me home?"

"Probably."

She laughed. "If you were Black, Preacher Daddy would like you."

"What's his opinion of Carleton?"

"He doesn't care for him."

"The two of you still together?"

"Not much. Is he the reason you're put off?"

The pink Jesus had tiny blue eyes. The nurse said they could see right through you. "I'm not put off."

"You're not quivering with excitement either."

"Give me time."

She climbed off Lenny's lap. "I changed my mind about the pizza. Preacher Daddy is expecting me home."

They passed the trailer and started up the hill to the village. Vickie pointed to the roadside. "Haley Flagg—the girl who disappeared—the woman who owns the Vintage Shop knew her, said she liked horses. Had special boots and britches to ride them."

❧

EXAMS ENDED. THE VILLAGE CLEARED OUT. Red hung a string of Santa faces across his window. Cliff wrote a feature about historic snowfalls that closed local businesses and canceled activities. He recounted his own fondness for watching snow falling on College Street and the elegant winter shadows of the ginkgoes.

Guests filled Sandy's house. Lenny made his way to the kitchen for a glass of chardonnay from one of the bottles in a tub of ice on the back porch. Zephyr joined him.

"When you're painting someone, do you talk much?"

"You have to. Sitting is tedious. Talk and music help pass the time. I'm a slow worker. There's a lot of time to pass."

"What about Haley? Did she talk about her family?"

"She didn't like the way her father got rich. He was driving, but the accident that killed her mother wasn't his fault. Bridge, ice, semi jackknifes, car skids sideway, truck slams into the passenger side. Fatal head injuries follow. He always had a spare woman around."

"How did her father get rich?"

"Mills. Minimum-wage employees. Socks, socks, and more socks. Real estate, too. Buying, selling, and financing property—mostly in low-income neighborhoods. She called him a swindler. Step-mommy had previously been Haley's weekend riding instructor. When Haley was in school, Daddy was fond of afternoon visits to the stables to discuss Haley's progress. A funeral. Six months later a marriage. Haley didn't appreciate the timing."

Lenny didn't recognize the woman scowling at Zephyr. Chemically refreshed blond curls. A ribbed sweater zipped up her throat. Too much eye shadow. She yanked Lenny's arm, demanded to know his name. He told her. She had heard of him, one of Bliss's toadies.

She pushed Lenny away and confronted Zephyr. "You...I gave you a photograph of my champion hound to paint, and you gave me a blotchy image of a dog pissing on a tree. You're a disgrace."

"*Blotchy*? Rather Cézanne-esque, I'd say."

"Grotesque, you mean."

"I never charged you a sou."

"I ought to *sue* you, asshole." She poured her plastic cup of beer down the front of Zephyr's pants.

He smiled at her. "May I get you another?" People laughed. The woman slammed the back door behind her.

"Josephine Mix," Zephyr said. "Biology." Someone handed him a towel. "I need a refill myself," he said.

Lenny worked his way from the kitchen to the front door. A few people were leaving. Sandy was wishing them good holidays. She turned to Lenny. "Wanted to tell you I hired Maisie Thorne to temp in the office over break. I had second thoughts, but two of my staff are out with flu and one is having a baby. I really need help to put things in order and she somehow appeared."

"*Somehow?*"

Sandy shrugged. "Don't ask."

"You work over break?"

"Always. Grades to record. Transcripts to prepare. Scholarships to adjust. Reports. What about you?"

"Filling in for someone. Security at the lake."

"Working for Warner?"

"You know him?"

"Dated him once. Long time ago. Nice guy—kind of bossy—but he preferred younger women. He was deeply offended when the school replaced football with soccer, which had been a club sport. Saved the college a ton of money."

Sandy followed Lenny down the street to where he had parked. "I considered buying a Jeep once, but it was too macho for me."

"Can be a chore to maintain," Lenny said.

"I wanted to tell you how much I've appreciated your work with Mr. Wallace. I've enjoyed our visits to the Cat as well." She squeezed Lenny's hand. "Since you mentioned Warner, I'll tell you something else. He has a talent for photography. Ask him and he'll tell you his subject is wildlife—birds especially. He explained to me about the lenses he uses, how they can capture details in the distance better than the eye can see them." Sandy lifted a leaf off the Jeep's hood. "The Bower kids…they're spoiled. They carry on. Another kind of wildlife for Warner to shoot."

She held the leaf over Lenny's head. "Not mistletoe, but it's what I've got." She brushed her lips across his. He watched her walk away and hoped someone would linger, help her clean up, share some wine, stay over. He remembered what waking up on Christmas morning to an empty house was like.

THE PRESTER MARKET was about to close. "Last-minute-last-minute gift?" The cashier had pinned floppy reindeer antlers to her red wool cap. She rang up a dozen packages of Nabs. "Or you going on a snacking spree?"

"Treat for my tenant," Lenny said.

"Long as I've been here and you been buying a bit of this, a dab of that, I wouldn't have guessed you got a tenant."

"More a nonpaying guest."

The clerk put the Nabs into a shiny red bag with a string handle and added a candy cane. "In case someone has a sweet tooth," she said.

The manager, thin face, long sideburns, frowned and followed Lenny to the door. "Happy Holidays," he said, turned the Open sign to Closed, and snapped the lock shut.

At home Lenny uncorked a Chianti that had been on sale. He sipped and heated beans and rice. Finished eating, he stacked his dishes to wash later. He wrote Merry Christmas on a Post-It and stuck it on the bag of Nabs.

A seasonable night. Low predicted around forty. He lifted the tarp, opened the Bug's door, and set the bag on the passenger's seat. Inside the trailer again, he settled into the chair, filled his wineglass, reread Capote's story "A Christmas Memory," filled his wineglass again, emptied it again, and fell asleep.

Christmas Day the wind turned south, and the last week of the year was warmer than normal. Not good, Mr. DeFoe said. No matter the weather there was always some sort of New Year's Eve gathering at the swimming beach, mostly older sons and daughters of residents, who were having their own celebrations. A balmy night would mean more underage consumption of alcohol and bad behavior than usual, not to mention careless fireworks. One or two people would go swimming or at least wade into water up to their waists. Lenny would not be welcome, but he was obliged to keep an eye on things.

The south wind, however, brought rain. When Lenny panned the beach with the dry cell lantern Warner always patrolled with, he saw only one couple huddled under a poncho. Others were partying in their cars. He told a boy parked in his parents' Chrysler to turn down his music. Donna McGoon leaned out of a Scout and offered Lenny a beer. If he would show up again at midnight, she would give him an unforgettable kiss. He declined the beer and said he'd think about the kiss. At midnight he was stopped on the roadside near Tittle's house, helping one of the residents change a tire. In the distance a firework popped, spattering tendrils of blue and red down the sky. Another fizzled and faded.

Lights went out, the new year settled in. The weather turned cold and windy.

Part II
The Gray Scale

I

"You're not Warner," the woman said.

Lenny glanced at measurements that Warner had marked on the doorframe. She stood five feet six, subtracting an inch for the heels of her black shoes. Her gray pantsuit lengthened her figure. A hundred and twenty pounds, Lenny guessed. Cropped hair. No jewelry, no makeup. Tanned face and hands. She was holding a folder.

"No ma'am. His office, his desk. He's taking some time off."

The woman stepped into the room and closed the door. "You are?"

"Leonard Grey—Lenny."

She opened the folder. "My notes say you occupy a trailer on Forest Road."

"I do."

"My name is Rose Bush. My parents thought they had a sense of humor. So did half the kids I grew up with. I kicked the ass of the last man who tried to be funny. I'm a private investigator. Mr. Flagg hired me."

"Warner should be back by next week."

"Call me Rose or Rosie. Don't mess with the Bush part. I mean that in every way possible." She sat down in the chair by the table with a stack of *Sports Illustrated* and opened the folder again. "You live near where Mr. Flagg's daughter was last seen."

"I do."

"Alone? You live alone?"

"I do."

"All these I do's. We need a preacher and a marriage license." She frowned and consulted her notes. "Are you acquainted with Clifford Barrow?"

"I know who he is. I'm not of his regular readers."

"I assume you're a student of some sort."

"I am."

"Mr. Barrow recently wrote about finding a crochet bag that reminded him of one Miss Flagg carried. Then a woman named Sandra Street told Mr. Barrow that someone took a ride in the MG car that used to belong to Haley." Rosie closed the folder and looked around. "What's with all these bird pictures on the walls?"

"Warner's hobby."

"He was good at it." She studied Lenny. "How old are you?"

"Twenty-five."

"I'm thirty-five. So we're not so far apart. My point is, I'm going to need someone I can confide in, run ideas past, someone I can been seen drinking with, blending in with. You don't have a girlfriend, do you?"

Lenny nodded at the folder. "I think you know the answer."

Rosie smiled. "You're right. Leonard Grey, sometimes seen in the company of a Black girl—Vickie something. Sometimes in the company of a white girl—Maisie Thorne. And every now and then at an establishment called the Cat with Sandy Street. I bet her parents thought they had a sense of humor too."

Lenny said, "You've been somewhere in the sun."

"My Tucson tan. Mr. Flagg hired me two weeks ago. I was recommended by his wife, who was a friend of a client whose cheating husband I had tracked down in Arizona."

"Who gave you information about me?"

"Cliff Barrow, of course."

Rosie scanned the room again. "Desk, chairs, filing cabinets. Toilet, I imagine, behind that curtain. Where does Warner cook and sleep?"

"A cottage on a lot at the far end of the lake, by the dam."

"He used to be a coach?"

"Long time ago."

"Fifty-five years old. Married, ever?"

"He never spoke of it."

Rosie stood up. "I'll be on my way then. I'm booked at the Sweeper Motel. Prester Inn would be more comfortable, but the motel is more interesting. I took a room in back where I can see who parks and uses the rear entrance. Love in the afternoon. I'm told faculty wives can be a frisky lot. What about Warner, any women in his life?"

"Sandy said she dated him once."

"What about you? I'm told the Black girl has a mean boyfriend."

"Carleton."

"Barrow told me the police suspected Carleton might have done harm to Haley, but nothing came of it. However, he has roughed up one or two young men who showed an interest in the Vickie person."

"I think I can outrun him."

"Bet you can't outrun me."

"What distance?"

"A mile?"

"What are we betting?"

"Bragging rights."

"I've been in Arizona. I'm not used to winter weather."

"The gym is deserted until the basketball teams return next week from break. There's an indoor track."

Rosie wrote the motel's phone number on her business card. "Room 109. Call a day ahead so I can dust off my Nikes."

Lenny closed the office and patrolled the east side of the lake. Mr. DeFoe flagged him down. He told Lenny the Residents' Association had voted to install a security gate at the entrance to the property. He reminded Lenny that the lake was going to be drained to treat invasive vegetation that had taken over areas near the shore. Lenny should prepare himself to deal with residents complaining about the smell and the sightseers. The gate wouldn't be finished in time to keep them out.

❧

"How come you have a key and permission to be in here?" Rosie asked.

"I tutor athletes."

"I heard people talking about some basketball player, how good he is."

"Wallace Wallace. He's one of mine."

The fluorescents flickered on. Rosie dropped her athletic bag by the starting line.

"I expected an old wooden track, loose boards and splinters," she said.

"State-of-the-art cement covered with carpet and a pad under it. Not much cushion. Ten laps to the mile."

"Take it easy on me. I'm out of shape and I haven't been sleeping much."

"Noisy motel?"

"Not sure. I've been staying with somebody."

They stretched and jogged, took off their warm-ups, and raced. Rosie led the first three laps. Lenny passed her and finished half a lap ahead. They shared a bottle of Gatorade and walked two laps to cool down. "Showers?" Rosie asked.

"I don't have access to the women's section. It's you and me in the men's."

"I'm okay with it," Rosie said.

"Not sure I am," Lenny said.

"Lenny, look all you want."

They undressed and showered. He asked how she got the scar on her thigh.

"Occupational hazard. I was chasing a guy across a rooftop and fell through a skylight. He was a serial rapist. A year later he tripped and tumbled down a flight of stairs. I survived. He didn't."

Lenny dried himself and turned his back while Rosie used his towel. "I believe justice finally wins out," she said. "But sometimes it needs a little push to make it over the finish line."

She didn't say anything more until they were in the Jeep. "The bag Barrow found was old, so the Vintage Shop seemed a likely place to check out. Kate, the woman who owns it, told me when her mother ran the business, Haley stopped in a couple of times. There was a Lalique perfume bottle she admired. I guess he was famous. Before she disappeared, she offered Kate a handsome pair of riding boots, but they weren't vintage, so Kate didn't buy them. Somebody bought the bottle."

"Anything else?"

"Kate mentioned the Harrisons."

"Zephyr Harrison painted Haley's portrait. He keeps it in case she returns and wants it."

"Does he think that's going to happen?"

"He believes what most people believe—Haley wanted a different life. He hopes she found what she was looking for and is happily alive somewhere."

"The bag, the MG incident—Mr. Flagg wants answers." Rosie elbowed the Jeep's door open. "Nice day. I'll walk."

"To the motel?"

She picked up her sports bag and slid down from the seat. "To Kate's."

❧

The note was taped to the trailer door: "Thomas is big on Christmas decorations. I'm not. They're still up. He's away. Professional meeting. I'm clumsy on ladders. Need help. Supper and wine to follow."

Lenny phoned Lia from Warner's office and explained days he was filling in for him. The association had hired a part-time night man, who came on at six. Lia reminded Lenny that ladders don't care what time it is.

Unstringing the garlands of holly from the wainscoting where Thomas had hung them took most of an hour. Lenny balanced on the ladder and removed the star from the top of the Fraser fir that was shedding its needles. Lia boxed up the ornaments she could reach.

He carried the ladder outside and left it in the garage. The Jaguar was there and a red Camaro. "A present to myself," Lia said. Maisie was using the Buick.

Lia handed Lenny a corkscrew and a merlot, one of Thomas's favorites. Lenny filled their glasses. She served the dinners—shepherd's pie, her specialty.

The house was warm. Lenny took off his sweater. Lia wasn't wearing much—minimal loungewear or pajamas. He wasn't sure and wasn't going to ask. He liked the shepherd's pie, and the wine, and the heat, and the scent of pine from the tree stripped of its ornaments, and Lia almost naked herself. Her skin retained its summer glow, courtesy of the salon popular with Prester students before spring break. She warned him not to lecture her on the dangers of tanning beds. Or alcohol, she said, opening another bottle.

They moved to the living room. Lia poked the embers in the fireplace and laid on more wood. Then Lenny was beside her on the couch, then he was lying down, his head in her lap, then she was kissing him, then he felt a hand under his thrift-shop shirt, fingers tracing the slopes of his skin, then...then he fell asleep.

When he sat up, Lia was sitting on the floor, gazing at the tiny flame flickering on the last piece of glowing wood.

"You know you talk in your sleep?"

"Did I say anything interesting?"

"You said 'please' a lot. The rest I couldn't make out—something you couldn't do either." She stared at the dying fire.

"Sometimes alcohol makes you want to do things, sometimes it keeps you from doing them. You agree?"

"I'll think about it."

"Lenny, you're quite a challenge."

❧

FRED DYE, THE NEW NIGHT MAN, left Lenny a note. Mr. Tittle complained the person who sullied his Cadillac may have done it again. Lenny warned himself to be courteous and helpful.

"Took your time getting here," Tittle said.

Lenny followed him to the garage. Tittle opened the back door of the Cadillac and pointed to crumbs on the seat. Lenny brushed them into the palm of his hand. Nabs, he thought.

"What are you going to do about it?"

"What do you want me to do?"

"File a damn report with the village police. Beef up the night patrol. Do your job."

"You said 'he.' You think your visitor was a man?"

"Or she. Don't know. Don't care. Just want the privacy and security I pay for—a hundred a month, Residents' Association dues." Tittle slammed the door shut. "Look at you—old jacket, jeans, and sneakers. At least Warner dressed the part, even carried a sidearm."

Tittle took a remote out of his pocket and closed the garage. "Side door doesn't lock. Needs a new one."

"I can replace it," Lenny said.

"Really?"

"I'll charge it to the association's account."

"What's your name again—Leonard something?"

"Grey."

"Mr. Grey, I appreciate your attention. Warner would have told me to change the lock myself."

"Part of the job."

"I hope that doesn't include sending you down with a mask and a wetsuit to open the dam and drain the lake."

"Mr. DeFoe hasn't mentioned it."

"Who knows, maybe they'll find a body or Indian artifacts or something."

"Over time most bodies float to the surface," Lenny said.

"You go to detective school?"

"I read it somewhere."

"There's a woman detective going around bothering people with questions about the girl who disappeared years ago."

"Did you talk to her?"

"I never met the girl."

"No, the detective."

"I'd have nothing to contribute," Tittle said and walked away.

Lenny drove to the village, bought a new lock, and decided to treat himself to a hamburger.

"Spent so much time over Christmas praying and listening to sermons that my knees and ass are still sore," Vickie said. She wrote Lenny's order on her pad. "If I had wanted sore knees and ass, I could have imagined better ways to get 'em."

She mixed his Coke and laid a straw on the counter beside it. "I'm off at two," she said.

"I need help."

"Doing what?"

"Handing me tools."

"I'd rather hand you something than take what Carleton hands me. He's mean lately. Some business scheme he's fretting about. The only Christmas spirit in him is from a bottle." She picked up Lenny's straw, nipped the end, and slowly peeled the paper back. "Ready for your sweet lips."

Lenny ate his burger and paid the check. Another hour before Vickie's shift ended. "Come on in," Sandy said and closed her office door. "Survive the holidays?"

"I met a detective."

"Who didn't? Miss Bush gets around. So do you. I heard your Jeep was parked quite late the other evening at the Thorne estate, and the professor was out of town."

"Who's your informant?"

"Maisie. She was going to pay mommy a visit but decided filial affection was not what mommy craved at the moment." Sandy smiled. Lenny sensed a question. "Did you?" she asked. He shook his head. "But you thought about it?"

Lenny had heard his mother tell him often enough, forget love, take what you can get. "Some," he said.

THIS TIME MRS. TITTLE ANSWERED the doorbell. Her husband had taken the Cadillac to visit Mr. DeFoe, something to do with Warner. DeFoe and some others were concerned.

She peered over his shoulder. Vickie stood in the driveway, holding Lenny's toolbox. "Under the circumstances be quick about your work."

Twenty minutes later, the new lock in place, Vickie waited in the Jeep while Lenny gave Mrs. Tittle the old lock and new keys. He walked back to car. She lingered in the doorway.

"What's she looking at?" Vickie asked.

"You," Lenny said.

He set his toolbox on the floor behind the seat. "Where to now?" Vickie asked.

"Parking lot, swimming beach."

"What you got in mind?"

"Walk up the hill to the dam."

"Going to drown me like in those old folk songs your people sing?"

"Last thing on my mind."

Before leaving, Warner had put up winter signs: *Open Noon to Dark. No Swimming. No Alcohol.* Lenny liked the extra money and didn't mind if Warner took his time coming home.

Vickie held Lenny's hand. The trash barrels and picnic tables were stored away until spring. The path to the dam had recently been cleared. He told her someone was going to put on a wetsuit and dive down to open the valve to release the water. She said, "Deep, dark water makes me sad."

"Why?"

"Don't know. What makes *you* sad?"

"Don't know either."

"Why did you bring me here?"

"Be alone with you."

"Your trailer would be warmer."

"I'm on duty."

"Lenny, what if we were standing outside Red's, people all around, and I asked you to kiss me. Would you?"

"Probably."

"I wouldn't bet on it."

"Are you in love with Carleton?"

"He's convenient. Sometimes he makes me happy."

"I'll take that bet—you and me in front of Red's."

"Sure you will. College Street is your territory. What about you in front of my house. Sidewalk, not in your car. People going by. Carleton, maybe."

"When?"

"Lord, Lenny, we're just talking. I should have kept my mouth shut."

"Not when you kiss me."

Vickie leaned over. "Give me a sample."

A minute later Vickie wiped her mouth. "Those white-boy lips, you know how to use them."

Lenny drove her home, she humming softly beside him.

Once I had wanted to be noticed. I dressed to show off my body. I imagined myself imagined by others, the willing starlet of fantasies, but they, the men who undressed me with their eyes, were the captives, captivated companions of mine. Basta. Enough. No more. I dressed in sexless clothes that hid my shape and imagined being a nun, a shadow shadowing the sidewalks and alleys, blessing the beggars begging, the mottled iguanas, the putas as they stared into mirrors and made up their faces for the night ahead.

Was I Catholic? Dobo asked. In one way or another, we all are, I said. The answer pleased him. Sí, verdad, *he said, and we shared a good bottle of rum.*

II

The afternoon sky was hazing over, a cold front on its way. Possibility of light snow. Maisie caught up with Lenny near the fountain between the quads. The water was turned off for winter, the marble swans usually bathed in mist stranded in pale solitude.

"Are we on speaking terms?"

"Sure," Lenny answered.

"No patrolling today?"

"President Bullard wants to see me."

"Something to do with basketball? Sandy said the team is ranked in the top twenty Division II schools. First time ever."

"You staying in school or dropping out?

"I signed up for lots of theater courses—history of Western drama, acting, writing—the whole bit. What about you? You need two courses to graduate."

"How do you know that?"

"Sandy's office has all the files. I know exactly how much money you still owe the school and how much it will cost to complete your coursework."

"What's the bottom line?"

"Two thousand. Can you swing that?"

"One, but not two."

"Listen, Lenny. There's a major donor to the college who might help you financially if you help him."

"Doing what?"

"He's never spelled it out, not to me, but he would be interested in discussing the matter with you." Lenny pushed his hands into his jacket pockets. "You're shivering."

"I'm cold."

"Perhaps you should ask that major donor for a pair of mittens."

❧

"BULLARD THANKED ME for Mr. Wallace passing English," Lenny said. "Called me a fine young man."

The Cat was almost empty. Sandy waved to a professor sitting at the table with his wife. "Know him?" she asked.

"Probably not the way you do."

"Are you referring to my statistical interest in noon-swim participants?"

"He likes to sun himself."

"Poly sci. Quite the brain, I'm told. Average in other ways. What else did Bullard say?"

"Sports are important to the whole fabric of the college."

"Meaning when our teams win, alums write checks."

"Speaking of money, I may need help paying my academic bills."

"Don't get ahead of yourself. You may or may not need extra assistance."

Sandy finished her drink and pointed to her empty glass. Lou was the name of the new bartender. Her black hair matched her slim trousers, her dark eyes her shirt, which was unbuttoned enough to show her lacy bra. She poured Sandy another vodka.

"Lenny, I'll tell you what I didn't before. In August Coach Bliss said he had a super recruit who would require tutoring to stay eligible, especially where writing was concerned. Could I recommend someone. I told him you had won the English department's essay prize two years in a row. That was enough to convince him. We talked about money. Officially, the athletic department can't pay you enough to cover what you need to graduate, but unofficially...I mean to say some of our loyal fans have deep pockets." She paused to let Lenny consider what she was saying and what she was implying.

"Anyway, if Prester qualifies for the national tournament, doors will open and you can walk right through and sign up to rent a cap and gown. You will remember forever standing in line for a cup of sweet punch on a hot June morning with the other graduates, sweating and posing for parents all smiles and cameras in hand. Who knows, a job might fall into your lap."

Lenny looked around the room for the server with impossibly tight leggings, then at Sandy again. "The alumni magazine interviewed me. It's doing a feature of Wallace and asked for my impressions. I told them he's a serious student and modest about his basketball skills."

"You realize that many alumni are not enthusiastic about sports. A few are downright opposed to anything but club and intramural competition. When you add the racial factor, there's another problem. I believe one of our state senators is deeply disturbed."

"I'm not sure how Wallace is going to do this term. I saw his class schedule. He has English I with Professor Hodges. He's not easy."

"Wallace's schedule has been revised. Oswald Fleck has kindly agreed to offer an independent study to fulfill Mr. Wallace's English I requirement."

"The department approved it?"

"Bullard suggested it. No one spoke against it."

"Is that—"

"Lenny, don't ask. Keep your head down. Doors will open. If Prester makes the tournament, DeFoe might give you a seat on the private jet he'll charter to fly his friends to the games."

"Who's the pilot—Bullard or Fleck?"

"Head down, Lenny. Head down."

THE TRACE OF SNOW OVERNIGHT melted in the morning. Lia took off her coat and draped it over a chair. "Lenny, this office is better than your moldy trailer. You should consider moving."

"I don't think Warner wants a roommate."

"Where is he?"

"Still on holiday."

"In January?"

"I expect him any day."

"Are you taking any courses or spending all your time patrolling the lake?"

"Two courses and working for athletics. If I'm not here, Mr. Dye is on call."

"What's with the water?"

"The lake is being drained."

Lia reached into her coat pocket and took out a package of Camels. "I came here to tell you Maisie's Bug has gone to the fender mender shop—or whatever."

"Tell me about the money."

Lia sighed and put the cigarettes away. "Maisie had some deal with Barrow, helping him do something. There must be more to it than that. I didn't ask for specifics. Where Maisie is concerned, I never do."

"What about her and Mr. Wallace?"

"Another one of her larks. She's more into music than sports. I think she has a dedicated table at Boxer's. Thomas listens to the games, though. He's interested in Mr. Wallace. The team averages eighty points a game, and Wallace and the other Black player account for more than half of those, mostly Wallace. Last year the team won seven games all season. So far this year it's undefeated."

"Mr. Wallace is special," Lenny said.

"Are you helping him or doing for him?"

"Helping."

"Thomas thinks you're doing."

"He's mistaken."

"I hope you're right."

WALLACE WAS A CELEBRITY, but the times Lenny saw him crossing the campus, he was alone. Someone had stolen his suede jacket. He hunched in a drab coat, a cap pulled low to hide his face. The more games the team won, the more invisible Wallace became, preferring the back row of classrooms, the side entrances to buildings, the back door of the gym.

He edged into the cubicle, dropped his backpack on the floor, and slumped into the chair. "Doctor Fleck is taking it easy on me this term. Good thing, too, because geography and biology have a lot of reading."

"Fleck doesn't make you write anything?"

"We talk about it more than doing it. Like how to organize an essay and shape paragraphs. You know—topic sentence and all that. Then he gives me writing samples to correct. He said it's a way for me to learn from other peoples' mistakes. Here..." Wallace opened his backpack, took out a folder, and handed Lenny a sheet of short paragraphs. Lenny looked at the one at the top of the page.

> Yesterday my friend, Nelson, and me went to the theater and seen Gone with the Wind. Its a story about the civil war. Atlanta, Georgia is where some of the action takes place. Bob my uncle lived there but when I visited him he didn't have much to say about the citys history.

"I'm supposed to find all the mistakes and fix them."

Lenny stood up and leaned over Wallace's shoulder. "Show me."

"Okay. *Me* should be *I*. *Seen* should be *saw*. *Civil war* should be capitalized. *Its* should have an apostrophe. *Citys* should too."

"Is Nelson the writer's only friend?"

"Probably not." Wallace studied the sentence. "Oh, it's one of those restrictive, non-restrictive places? No commas?"

"No commas. Any places there should be commas?"

"After *Bob* and after *uncle*."

"Keep looking."

"After *him*."

"Where else?"

"Don't know."

"After *Georgia* and after *there*. Fleck might argue for after *yesterday*, but that's debatable. What about the punctuation of movie and book titles?"

"Don't know, but I'll look it up. Fleck made me buy a handbook full of rules. I fall asleep reading it. I wish he'd show me where the mistakes are. Then I could puzzle out how to fix them and hunt up the rule to see if I got it right—you know, find the rule and read up on it." Wallace shook his head. "But I'm supposed to guess what's wrong and keep reading till I find the rule to fix what I guess is wrong. Confusing, ain't it?"

Lenny had an idea. "What about this—first, I write down the pages in the handbook you should read, and then you apply what you've read to correcting the mistakes."

"Like you find the mistakes and tell me what pages in the handbook to read so I can find the mistakes on my own and correct them?"

"I think we're saying the same thing."

"People think I'm dumb. They don't say it, but I know what they're thinking. I can read their faces. I'm Black and I don't talk like they do. Some on the team, they laugh at me behind my back. Rooster is the worst."

"*Rooster?* You mean Roister?"

"That's his name, but nobody calls him that. He played at some fancy school in Virginia and expected he be starting, but I'm in his place. He's always saying stuff or doing stuff. He wouldn't admit to it, but he put a bar of lye soap in my locker with a note telling me that if I scrubbed hard enough, it might make my skin white. The next day in practice I shot him a pass. He wasn't paying attention. The ball almost bust his nose."

"Anything you do for fun?"

"Don't have time."

"Even for Vickie?"

"Carleton is first team there. For all I know, you're second. Anyway, I don't have leisure to socialize." Wallace tucked the paper with the sentences into the folder and zipped up his backpack. "Got to meet a man from the Raleigh paper in Coach's office. I think Coach likes the publicity more than I do."

Sandy had left a note in Lenny's Jeep. She was seated at the bar in the Cat, waiting for him.

"You could have phoned the athletic department. One of the secretaries would have given me your message."

"Lenny, I'm beginning to wonder if we should even meet here, in public."

"What's up?"

"Not sure, but I sense trouble. The provost's secretary stopped by my office and asked to see your records. The next day she was back again wanting to see everything in our files about Mr. Wallace."

"He had a forty-point game in Greensboro the other night."

"Don't interrupt. Then yesterday I saw Maisie Thorne getting into a new VW. A loaner from a body shop, she said." Sandy pushed her glass aside. "A fiftyish white guy was with her. Wore an expensive suit. She didn't say where she had borrowed him. I heard him tell Maisie he needed to get back to Raleigh." Sandy picked up the check. "Do body shops give customers new cars to drive?"

"Not usually," Lenny said.

Outside, she pulled her coat tightly around her. "MGs aren't great for heat. At least the days are getting longer."

III

"You need a lock on your door," Rosie said. "And a phone. I could have called instead of driving over here."

"If I had a lock, you would have waited in your car instead of enjoying the comfort of my trailer."

"Cold comfort. This place is freezing."

"The space heater works fast."

"I'm not intending to stay—thank you."

"You're not here to be my valentine?"

"That's next week. I'm here to tell you something. Carleton Pyle brought an item to Kate's shop today, a perfume bottle he thought was old and wanted to know if it was worth anything, the same bottle Kate told me about and I told you. Kate reminded him that the store sold clothes, not glass or ceramics, and pretended not to remember it. Then he said the bottle had come from the store in the first place, that a man had bought it and given it to a woman he liked, and she had given it to him—Warner to Haley Flagg to Carleton."

"Haley Flagg gave it to Carleton, or he took it?"

"Gave, I bet."

"Because?"

"Lenny, think. You're a white girl who wants to live a whole different life from the privileged one you know. What would really push your family away—sex, but not with anyone, with a no one—a *Black* no one with a reputation for being on the wrong side of the law."

"And in gratitude for the pleasure, Haley gave Carleton the bottle?"

"She was planning on leaving town, why not? Tell me about this Warner guy."

"You tell *me*. I'm sure you've been investigating."

"Fifty-five years old. In charge of security at a private lake. Years ago was assistant football coach at the college. Not happy when the school dropped the sport. Never married. Likes to date younger women. Quiet. Generally, well-liked. Hobby is nature photography. Mostly birds. From time to time he hunts or shoots targets with some country old-timers whose families have been here forever and don't favor what academic types refer to as changing demographics—Black people and Yankees moving in. By the way, he's been gone a long time, hasn't he?"

"More than anyone expected. Have you been investigating me?"

"Wasn't easy, much of your life being lived in Maine. Folks there tend to be reluctant to give out information, especially long distance."

"Not much to give out."

"You were a good student and ran track. Your girlfriend's name was Jessica. Your father died. Your mother clerked in a grocery. You had a friend named Tommy Hall. He runs his father's business, selling boats and trailers of various kinds. His father sold your mother a small Airstream. She parked it on her lawn by her woodpile. Never moved it. Neither Tommy nor his father understood why she wanted it."

"Privacy."

"Tell me about Jessica."

"She ran cross country."

"Let's get personal. You have sex with her?"

"Yes."

"With anyone else?"

"She did. I didn't."

"How did you feel about that?"

"Her choice."

Rosie pinched her lip and stared at Lenny. "Say more. When did it start, when did it end?"

"September senior year, fooling around on the team bus on the ride back from a meet. Probably Brunswick. Three months later. Portland. Christmas. I drove her to the doctor's office. The other guy paid and drove her home."

"Whose child?"

"His."

"How was that decided?"

"I always wore something. He didn't."

"Now, years later, what do you feel?"

"Guilt."

"Why? The baby wasn't yours."

"At the doctor's office she asked me to stay with her. I didn't."

"Would it have made any difference?"

"She needed a friend. People said things. She moved away and went to cosmetology school. She'd planned to attend college."

"What about the other guy?"

"He went into the timber business with his father."

Rosie smiled. "Okay then. One more question. Why did your mother need a trailer for privacy?"

"Sometimes she wanted to entertain a friend. I was a light sleeper."

"And here you are in another Airstream."

"It's what I can afford. Don't play therapist."

DEFOE SAID, "I saw the PI's car in your yard last night. When she came to my house, she said, 'I'm Rose.' She mumbled the Bush part. I don't blame her. *Rosie Bush.* I bet the boys had fun with that."

They stood on the shore and gazed at the nearly empty lake. DeFoe carried a trash bag in one hand and pointed with the other. "For about thirty yards the bottom is dry enough to walk on. After that it's too sloppy. We're paying a crop duster to fly over and spray to kill off the vegetation."

They heard footsteps and turned around. "Got something?" Cliff asked.

"Otherwise, I wouldn't have phoned." DeFoe took a boot out of the bag. "Found it yesterday."

He held up the boot for Cliff to examine. "Green and slimy, not much to look at. Its mate is probably somewhere close."

"How come it stayed under water?" Cliff asked.

"Rocks," DeFoe said.

"How far down?"

"Three feet, maybe. If the lake weren't always so weedy and silty, one of the residents sailing their Sunfish like they do might have seen the boot on the bottom."

Lenny said the boot looked like one of the pair Haley wore in the photograph Miss M took.

"Of course it's hers," Cliff said.

"I suppose the boot is evidence. The police will want it."

"Evidence of what, Wade? There was no crime. Haley Flagg sold her stuff, left town, and moved somewhere she didn't want people to find her."

"Chief Pritchard and some others might see it differently."

"What others? Weaver, Bullard, even my editor—the party line is nothing bad happens at the college or in the village. No crime. Everything is peaceful and fulfilling. If someone is attacked one foot outside the village limits, then it happened someplace else. Might as well be in another state, another country."

"Cliff, your cynicism runneth over."

"I'm a giving person." He looked at Lenny again. "From what I hear, so are you—giving that Black Mr. Basketball a lot of help so he can stay in school and strut his stuff."

DeFoe shook his head. "Cliff, meeting adjourned. Here, you take charge of the boot. Write about it, give it to the police, or do what you think you should. I would prefer you not publicize draining the lake. We don't need a lot of people wanting to walk in the mud, hunting for whatever."

"Find anything else besides empty bottles and condoms?"

"None of the latter, a few of the former, and several pairs of sunglasses."

Cliff trudged back to his car, the bag with the boot under his arm. "What about the rocks?" Lenny asked.

"They look like ones at Warner's place. I gave them to Professor Prescot. He teaches the rocks-for-jocks course. Be interesting if they were special."

The sun was bright now. The houses on the hillside glowed in the light. Lenny thought of the estates where he grew up, a cluster of Queen Annes called the "villas" perched on the headland overlooking the harbor. A girl named Gretchen had invited him to hers for a birthday party, but he didn't go. He had seen Gretchen's father's car parked late at night by his mother's teardrop Airstream.

"Lenny, I spoke with Coach Bliss. He mentioned a meeting—some sort of faculty committee. He's concerned."

"I'm invited," Lenny said. Gretchen warned him he'd regret not coming. He had no choice this time.

⁂

EIGHT MEN SPREAD THEMSELVES around the seminar table in the paneled room in Mori Hall. Quigley, the college provost, sat at the opposite end from Lenny and called the meeting to order. He introduced the others: Maynard, econ; VanNoy, chemistry; Crainshaw, biology; Edgar, math; Brooks, Romance languages; Thorne, history; Harrison, art.

Quigley said the committee had questions and concerns regarding the assistance Lenny was paid to provide some of the athletes, specifically Mr. Wallace Wallace. Was Lenny prepared to answer their questions truthfully?"

Dressed in his best jeans and a flannel shirt, Lenny answered that he was.

Edgar interrupted to inquire if Lenny was paid by the hour or by the number of students he tutored and, in either case, how much he received.

"Five dollars and fifty cents per hour," Lenny said.

Edgar quipped that he had earned a buck-fifty an hour busing tables at MIT in his student days.

"Moving along," Quigley said. "We're curious about certain assignments." He opened a folder and took out several sheets of paper. One was passed down the table to Lenny. "According to Miss Crawley, the English department secretary, Professor Fleck gave Mr. Wallace two or three of these pages every week. They contain short paragraphs filled with mistakes—grammar and punctuation. Mr. Wallace was supposed not only to correct each mistake but also identify where in the course handbook the error and proper usage are discussed."

"Sounds a bit de trop," Brooks mumbled.

Quigley continued. "Do I have it right, Mr. Grey?"

"Yes."

"Which handbook, Mr. Grey?"

"*Little, Brown*."

"I think mine was *New Century*," VanNoy commented.

Crainshaw nudged VanNoy's arm. "Nineteenth, I suppose."

"Gentlemen," Quigley said, "please." He stared at Lenny. "Mr. Grey, certain page numbers, probably referring to the handbook, are written neatly in ink in the margins on of the page Fleck gave Mr. Wallace. The corrections, written in pencil, are a bit sloppy. I—we—assume you're the neat ink hand and Mr. Wallace is the sloppy pencil hand."

"Yes," Lenny said. "I'm sure Professor Fleck knew my handwriting. I wasn't trying to deceive anyone."

Quigley stared at the freshly painted ceiling, then down at Lenny again. "Mr. Wallace didn't exactly fulfill the assignment himself—correct? You identified the appropriate handbook references, not Mr. Wallace."

"I pointed him toward the rules. He read them and made the corrections."

"But he didn't find the rules himself."

"No."

"Wasn't finding the rule part of the assignment?"

"It shouldn't have been."

"Why do you think so?"

"Wallace would read the paragraph. Sometimes he immediately saw what needed correcting and could find the handbook reference by himself. He didn't need my help or the handbook's. If he didn't see what was wrong, my references to the handbook guided him. I didn't make the corrections for him. I pointed him in the right direction. He read the handbook and—"

"Read where you told him to read it."

"Yes, but—"

"But no. You were essentially finding for him what he was assigned to find for himself."

"Excuse me. If a person doesn't recognize an error, how can he be expected to find a rule about it in a handbook? At least I got Wallace to read it, understand what he read, and correct what needed correcting."

Quigley raised his hand. "All right. All right. Next..." He opened another folder and took a deep breath. "Fall semester students in Professor Fleck's remedial class were assigned a book report. Each could select one of three short novels—*The Old Man and the Sea, Ethan Frome,* or *Portrait of the Artist as a Young Man*. Mr. Wallace chose the Hemingway."

"*Ethan Frome*. Who wrote that?" Maynard asked.

Quigley blinked and looked at Lenny. "Edith Wharton," Lenny said.

"Yes, of course," Quigley said. He passed a page down the table, the report Lenny had written. "A very slim report, Mr. Grey. Wouldn't you agree?"

"I would."

"Did *you* write it?"

"Yes."

"The style, I suppose, is intended to imitate Mr. Wallace's."

"Yes."

"Rather well done," VanNoy said. "Could have fooled me."

A harsh glance from Quigley. The page made its way back to him. "Mr. Grey, you wrote Mr. Wallace's assignment for him and attempted to obscure the fact by writing poorly in the manner one would have expected had Mr. Wallace written it himself."

"Yes."

Quigley replaced the page in the folder and tapped it sharply on the table. "Mr. Grey, although it may be what—six years—since you matriculated, perhaps you recall signing the pledge neither to give or receive aid on tests and examinations and that all written work be that of the student submitting the work in his or her name."

"Mr. Wallace didn't submit the report. I did."

"Please, Mr. Grey, no sophistries. He permitted the work to be submitted on his behalf. His permission counts as his cooperation and collusion to subvert the literal wording of the rule and his intent to cheat."

Quigley took off his glasses and rubbed his eyes. "However, we concede there is a—if you will excuse me—gray area and instead of expelling Mr. Wallace—"

"Wait. I believe the report Mr. Wallace wrote was misplaced or lost and somehow someone else's report took its place, work that wasn't Wallace's but was stapled to a page with his name on it. When I realized the report wasn't his, I tried to write the one he wrote, which he gave to someone to type. I was his tutor, so I had seen his first draft and could go from there."

"Mr. Grey, let me understand. This hocus-pocus you refer to occurred between Wallace giving his work to a typist and thereafter?"

"I believe so."

"I don't. You can't have Wallace's original report mysteriously disappearing and your report imitating Wallace's writing take its place. And what about the report you suggest was mistakenly attributed to Wallace?"

"I'm only guessing there was a mix up at some point. Eventually, the report Mr. Wallace wrote found its way into Professor Fleck's possession and earned a passing grade."

"If your imitation is accurate, I can only wonder what standard the professor goes by."

"Where are we then?" Brooks asked.

"In the dark," Harrison said.

"That's not a racial comment, is it?" Edgar asked.

Quigley rapped the folder on the table again. "Gentlemen, please." He focused on Lenny. "The only path through the misdirection and ambiguities involved in this matter is the one we agreed on before. To assuage faculty doubts, or worse, an investigation by the NCAA, we shall allow Mr. Wallace to withdraw after the fact from the remedial English course in question and do so without blemish on his record. However, without credit for remedial English, he is not eligible to take English I, which leaves him presently enrolled in two courses, one short of Prester's requirement for being a full-time student and the NCAA's eligibility requirement to compete in intercollegiate sports. It may also affect his scholarship to attend the college—"

"If he stays," Harrison said.

"Precisely," Quigley said. "If he stays..."

Seven men avoided looking at Lenny.

"Now, Mr. Grey, we come to you—another gray area, I'm afraid. You are, of course, no longer employed by Prester in any position. You may go about pursuing your degree without prejudice as far as the college is concerned. Make sure to return your parking permit along with the key to your cubicle, if you have one."

Lenny pushed back from the table. "Are we finished then?"

"We are, but I anticipate a substantially different reaction from the student body once news of Mr. Wallace's situation is bruited about. My knowledge of basketball is limited, but I'm told that Prester's chances of winning its remaining games and the conference are slim now and postseason play is out of the question."

Thomas Thorne walked with Lenny slowly across campus. "Quigley is the college provost, although he acts as if he's the president. Weeks ago, Edgar, I, and the others were curious about Wallace and what seemed to us to be a new era of recruiting athletes in general and Wallace in particular. None of the committee admires Bullard and his leadership. Wallace became our focus. It wasn't personal, not for us. Except for Quigley, the committee approved of the job you were doing in general with the athletes you work with, and we suspected we didn't know the whole story about the book report and the surprising honor Bullard bestowed on Professor Fleck. I still don't think we have all the facts. I'm sure there is something you haven't told us. Care to comment?"

"No."

"If it's any consolation, sooner rather than later Bullard is going to receive a no-confidence vote from faculty council." They stopped at College Street. "Valentine's Day, Leonard. Anyone special in your life?"

"Not this year," he said.

LOU POURED TWO RIOJAS for Lenny to sample. Sandy sipped her favorite vodka. He handed her the card—outside, a red heart on a white background. Inside, "To My Valentine" and a smaller heart. Thank You written in blue ink. "It was lying on my bed when I came home from my get together with the provost. It didn't go well."

"Lenny, I'm sorry. I don't know what else to say."

"The choice was mine. I insisted on rewriting Wallace's assignment. I turned in work I wrote in his name. Someone's head has to roll. You warned me."

"Without the tutoring money, can you manage?"

"Not sure if Mr. DeFoe and the Residents' Association will continue my employment until Warner returns. Otherwise, I'll find enough odd jobs to keep me busy and put Nabs on my table." He held up his glass to the light. "Have to cut back on pricey Riojas."

"I'll figure something out."

"Figure how Quigley collected his evidence and what Cliff Barrow's role was."

"We can be sure what the subject of his next column will be. The only question is will he concentrate on you and Bliss, or will he try to go after Bullard and the misguided alumni who place athletics above scholarship. A few issues ago he asked how many believed that if the library were burning, the field hands would rush from the gym to put it out. We're going to be treated to more of the same."

Lenny noticed Lou's puzzled expression and turned around. Smith was behind him.

"Lenny, Wade DeFoe said I might find you here. He was passing your trailer. He saw smoke. He got to a phone as quick as possible. Sorry, but nothing could save your trailer. Nothing."

❧

TEN O'CLOCK. Lenny parked in a space behind the motel. Rosie had given him her key. She was sleeping at Kate's. Someone might as well use the motel room. She'd put it on her expense account.

Lenny had followed Smith to the trailer, the hulk left of it. Tittle, the Harrisons, and a few other Bower residents had heard sirens and driven over to see what was happening. Lenny spent an hour with Smith, staring at the debris and watching the village fire chief take photographs. Unlocked door—easy for anyone to get inside, splash some gasoline around, and light a match. Any insurance? You know the answer, Lenny said.

"Here, found this." The chief handed Lenny the bracelet he had forgotten about. "Didn't melt. A little scrubbing, it will be shiny as new."

Sandy alerted Rosie. They took Lenny to Lindy's Diner and bought him supper. Students sitting nearby were arguing whether Wallace had been set up or led astray. And who was the tutor? They didn't know his name, but they'd heard about the fire. The basketball season was up in flames, why not where the tutor lived? Whatever his name, he fucking deserved what he got.

Sandy followed Lenny and parked her car beside his. "Need help carrying your luggage, sir?" she said, trying to make him smile. She followed him inside and waited in the corridor while he unlocked the door and turned on a light. Chair, table, TV, bed. The air seemed as gray as his mood.

"Want me to stay—just talk?" she asked. Lenny shook his head. "I'm not sure how all the pieces fit," she continued, "but I'd avoid campus for the rest of the semester. I'll arrange for you to withdraw from the two courses you're taking and refund any fees you've paid. You can finish your course work in summer school."

Lenny shook his head again. "Also," Sandy said, "I'd keep my door locked."

In the morning Lenny replenished his wardrobe at the Graham Goodwill.

"Lenny, you sure you want to work today?" Mr. DeFoe asked.

"Nothing better to do," he said.

"Lenny, Warner's not coming back. He died. The sheriff of Fremont County, Wyoming, contacted our police department. A rancher had found a body in a tent along some river and the sheriff identified the victim from his driver's license—our

Warner. He'd been drinking—steadily, apparently. Spent all afternoon at a bar in a town named Dubois, which, I guess, is in Fremont County, and took a couple of bottles of whiskey with him. The sheriff thinks he passed out and froze to death. Ten below zero, a tent, no fire, no heat, nothing but a sleeping bag. Perhaps not a bad way to go."

"Think that's what he wanted?"

"For months we'd discussed draining the lake. He wasn't in favor. He said he didn't want to be around when it happened."

"So he went to Wyoming?"

"Wasn't the first time. He told the bartender in Dubois about working one summer when he was seventeen on a road crew, how he liked open spaces, trout fishing, and all the elk."

"Was he planning to come back here?"

"Before he left, Warner had some tests. His doctor hadn't told him yet, but he had some variety of lung cancer. He used to be a smoker. I suspect Warner knew he was sick. He certainly coughed a lot. I'm not sure he had any plans."

"What happens now?"

"We continue your employment. The cottage Warner lived in belongs to the Residents' Association. It goes with the job. Chief Pritchard is going to want to search Warner's stuff. The boot in the lake is going to play tricks with the chief's mind. The rocks in the boot match the ones in Warner's yard. When the official search is finished, I'll have a crew clean up the cottage and store Warner's things, then you can move in. You'll probably need to bunk at the motel four or five more nights."

Lenny sat in the chair. Rosie propped herself in the middle of the bed, pillows behind her back.

"Warner lit out for Wyoming because he knew when the lake was drained, the boot would be discovered, and he was the one who weighted it with rocks and threw it into the water?"

"It's possible," Lenny said.

"How? The morning she was standing on the roadside thumbing a ride, Officer Smith didn't see any riding boots. If Warner happened by, picked her up, and killed her—which is what Pritchard must be thinking—what's her boot got to do with it? And if he killed her, what happened to the body?"

"Why didn't he want the lake drained?"

"The lake is a dumb place to try to hide a corpse. It can be done, but amateurs usually screw it up. And no body was found. The diver searched the deepest part by the dam. All the rest is visible. If Pritchard thinks Warner was full of guilt for killing Haley and headed west and drank himself into a stupor intending to die, it won't hold water, so to speak. Cancer is more likely a motive for taking the freezy way out."

Rosie looked at Lenny. "Made you smile."

"I can see why Kate likes you."

"Sweetie, it's not about my wit."

Rosie twisted around and rearranged the pillows. "My back can't take much more of this. It's dark outside. I'm hungry. My expense account is ready, willing, and able."

Head down, Lenny followed Rosie into the Cat. The hostess led them to a table in the farthest corner from the bar. He glanced at the menu and closed it. Rosie told him he had to eat more than a salad. He ordered paella and whatever white wine Lou wanted to send over.

When the server brought a verdejo, he said that one of the patrons at the bar had seen Lenny come in and wanted to give him a complimentary banana, but the kitchen was out of them. The server apologized and left.

"I don't understand."

"Cliff's Notes." Rosie opened her handbag and gave Lenny the newspaper.

> Years ago, my uncle Rupert had saved enough from pig farming to take a vacation. Producing pork was good business then, and farmers like Rupert, though looked down upon as uneducated hoi polloi by the Prester faculty and scorned by assorted local nabobs, had real money in their pockets. Rupert wanted to visit a foreign country. Canada was cold. Mexico wasn't. The southeast coast was recommended. Plenty of opportunities to observe Mexican agriculture and avoid expensive tourist attractions.
>
> Rupert had never been to a zoo and never seen lions or tigers or giraffes and such. He didn't see any in the Mexico either, but he saw plenty of monkeys. The squat concrete hovels the natives lived in lacked screens—and window glass as well—allowing monkeys to swing in to visit whenever they wanted. Cuddly and cute from a distance, the creatures were not that welcome. Besides hiding bugs and vermin in their hair, they were dirty and destructive, and the males tended to masturbate frequently. Rupert was content to observe moneys from a distance.
>
> Soccer, of course, was the sport Mexican children played, kicking a scuffed ball in the dusty roadways, little more than cart paths. Outside several hovels, Rupert was surprised to see rims and frayed nets or bottomless produce baskets nailed to poles or tree trunks—basketball courts, if you will. Instead of kicking the scuffed ball, children threw it.
>
> But wait. Rupert stopped in his tracks. He saw a large monkey darting in and out of gaggle of shouting children, and much to Rupert's amazement, the monkey lofted the ball with unerring accuracy at the basket. The monkey could do all sorts of tricks with the ball, passing it behind his back, dribbling it, balancing it on his head.
>
> Rupert—bless his heart—was not immune to the virus of greed. He could make the monkey a star, put on halftime exhibitions in college gyms and arenas. Baskets for bucks. He approached

the man who qualified as the monkey's owner because he let the animal eat from his banana tree and had fixed it a place to sleep. Rupert offered to purchase the critter. The owner, however, made an unexpected request: Rupert had to teach the monkey how to read and write.

Rupert assured the man that he lived near a prestigious college where finding a tutor for the monkey would be no problem. Did the animal have a name? Mono is the Spanish word for monkey. This one was called Mono Mono because he was twice what an ordinary monkey was.

Rupert acquired a crate. A doctor tranquilized Mono Mono for traveling, and days later it was living in a cage on a farm in North Carolina. Eventually, Rupert would surround a grove of trees with netting to allow Mono Mono more room to swing and climb and be himself. He also poured cement to create a basketball court and erected a goal to official standards. Several times a day Mono Mono played with a regulation ball to his heart's content.

The president of the college heard about Mono Mono and came to witness with his own eyes the creature's incredible skills. Indeed, presenting Mono Mono at halftime events would be financially rewarding to both Rupert and the college. Rupert joked with the president that the monkey's previous owner would reclaim Mono Mono if Rupert failed to keep his promise that the monkey would learn to read and write.

Ridiculous, the president said. Monkeys aren't literate. Ours will be, Rupert said. Anyone dumb enough to make such a request was dumb enough to believe examples of Mono Mono's writing mailed to him from the college were proof the monkey could read and write.

Basketball season started. Mono Mono put on extraordinary halftime shows. Crowds like never before paid to attend. Perhaps inspired by Mono Mono, now the college's mascot, the team was undefeated. The college president appointed a scholarship student to write little paragraphs of simple prose to send to the previous owner. All was well until the student demanded more money. Affronted by such ingratitude, the president refused. In the dark of night, the student tore down the netting and let Mono Mono escape.

Months later Mono Mono reappeared. Chained to the belt of a new owner, who played an accordion, the monkey wandered a city sidewalk, holding out a tin cup.

All in all, Rupert believed he had given Mono Mono a better life. In my opinion, *ignorantia sit beatitudo.*

"I never asked for more money," Lenny said.

The server brought Rosie's desert and more wine for Lenny. "At least you're employed and have a place to live," she said between bites of flan. She offered him a taste. "What's happening to Mr. Wallace?"

"He's barely passing his two courses. Mr. DeFoe wants him to withdraw and attend an accredited program in Florida that specializes in improving athletes' academic skills. If Wallace agrees and reapplies to Prester, DeFoe will pay the program's fee. It isn't cheap."

"Maybe Wallace will learn what *ignorantia sit* whatever means."

"That's kind of a reach."

"What *does* it mean?"

"Ignorance is bliss."

❧

THE HALLWAY SMELLED OF DISINFECTANT. The ice machine grumbled. A Do Not Disturb sign hung on Lenny's door. It opened. "Where you been?" Vickie asked. "I waited over an hour."

"How..."

"Don't stare like I got two heads or something." Lenny sat down on the edge of the bed. "A friend works here. She let me into your room. I saw you drive up. That lady in the car, she's the one going around asking questions."

"Rosie."

Vickie sniffed. "You been drinking?"

"Some."

"Been doing anything else?"

"No."

"You want more? I know you like wine. Don't know what flavor, but I brought a bottle. We could pass it back and forth like those sad folks do up at the old graveyard behind the car wash."

Vickie took the bottle out of her coat pocket and unscrewed the cap. Lenny tasted and made a face.

"That good, huh? Let me sample." She did and made a face. "You're not going to fall asleep, are you?"

"I might," Lenny said.

"Don't. As Preacher Daddy preaches, the good time is upon us. We must use it wisely. Tonight he's at some meeting in Alabama, and mama's visiting her sister in Georgia."

Vickie wore a beige sweater, slacks, and heels. She kicked them off and pulled the sweater over her head. She knelt in front of Lenny. "Unhook me, please." Her breasts fell loose. Then she stood in front of him, inching her slacks over her hips.

"Got to pee," Lenny said. When he came back, Vickie was waiting for him in bed.

Later she said, "I'm flooding over. You must have been saving up one long time." She nestled against Lenny. They both fell asleep. Next morning the trash truck woke him. Seven o'clock. Vickie was gone. The night before might have been a dream, but the sheet said otherwise.

Lenny found the note in his Jeep.

Mr. Leonard, I see you again but it will be some while. Prester don't agree with me, least so right now. You my friend, and I don't hold nothing against you for what all happened. Don't care for Rooster much, but I will miss the rest of the team. Mr. DeFoe wants me to attend a program in Florida. Said it will make me smart. Or smarter, the comparative. I wouldn't know that except for you. I do like learning things. It's important. I like writing too. So I'll probably go like he wants. Coach Bliss was always talking about his philosophy, winning. Mine is Keep On and that's what I intend to do, Keep On.

Sincerely,

Wallace Wallace

THE *VIEW* NOTED THE ABSENCE of Wallace Wallace from the team lineup and published Lenny's photograph. Conversations at the lunch counter faded, heads turned, customers watched him sit down. Dr. Teddy patted Lenny's shoulder and whispered, It will pass.

Vickie winked and took Lenny's order. She tore off a page from her pad and palmed him a note—I can still smell you on me. When she brought him ketchup for his hamburger, he said he would pick her up at three.

Spring was early. Daffodils about to bloom. Lenny parked in front of Vickie's house. She said, "Remember our bet?"

A school bus rasped to a stop. The children pointed and laughed at Lenny and Vickie standing in the street kissing. The bus left, trailing pungent exhaust behind it. Vickie disappeared into her house. The car that was stopped behind the bus didn't move. Carleton leaned out the window. "Preacher Daddy ain't going to like you putting on a show in public."

Carleton pulled his car to the curb and got out, all six feet and two hundred pounds of him, dressed in a tan suit and a white shirt open at the collar. He had turned down a chance to play football at one of the state's Black colleges. The scars across his cheek suggested other activities. A gold stud shone in his ear. Dark eyes. A wide nose. Fifteen years older than Vickie, but Lenny could see why she was attracted to him.

"Vickie and I had a bet," Lenny said.

"Bet you she had more than that. Don't imagine she visited the motel just to catch some Z's."

"Is she what you want to talk about?"

"No, me and her is finished. I apologized for not treating her right. I drink sometimes and get a little rough. But I'm a different man now—*Mr. Pyle* unless I say to call me Carleton. I'm partners with Mr. Dodson. The court decided I own the land my grandaddy farmed, own it free and clear, no debts, all taxes paid. Dodson and I agreed to put our properties together and build houses, create a mini subdivision. Won't have a lake, but some fine homesites."

Vickie came out of her house and stared at Carleton dressed in his suit. She smiled. "You're on your way," she said.

"Baby, going to be somebody."

"You stop by to tell me *that*?"

"I saw you and saw who was driving. I wanted to tell him what I didn't tell that woman who's been asking questions. I can explain about the boot. Warner and me had history. None of it good. I hear he's dead now, so it won't matter to him what I did." Carleton watched a girl circling the block on her bike.

"Warner liked 'em young and pretty. That's what Haley was. You know who I'm talking about?"

"I do," Lenny said.

"She was polite but didn't care for him. I told the detective woman about the perfume bottle Haley admired and how Warner bought it for her and she gave it to me after we... enjoyed each other's company. She'd been camping out on my granddaddy's property, leaving her old life, giving stuff away—going free, she called it.

"The day before she planned to thumb a ride and head on out, Warner paid her a visit. She was too shaken up to leave that day. She camped another night and wrote me a note about what happened and put the note in one of her riding boots, which she left where I would find it. Never understood why there wasn't a pair of boots, but there wasn't. Time went by. When Haley's family couldn't find her, I made up my mind. I'd lost Haley's note, so I didn't have her own words. I decided on an indirect approach.

"Warner patrolled a lot and residents were always watching who visited, especially if the visitor was Black. I knew a man who tended several residents' property—cutting grass, cleaning gutters, those kinds of chores. He did some work at Warner's place and noticed rocks, pretty ones, that Warner had around a birdbath. People were used to seeing the man's truck and thought nothing about it. He let me borrow it. I took some of the rocks, crammed them into Haley's boot and drove around the other side of the lake to where the Hubbards lived. The man told me they were away. I slung the boot as far as I could into the lake and left. When someone found it, police might start investigating Warner, might discover that what he liked about his job was spying on girls skinny dipping or smoking dope or having sex. Rumor was he had a special camera and took their pictures."

The door to Vickie's house opened. A man in black trousers and a white shirt looked out—Preacher Daddy, Lenny thought. Vickie waved, but he just stood there, watching.

"Problem was," Carleton said, "I expected someone would find the boot, but no one did. In my mind I went back and forth about what to do and never decided. I guess time decided for me."

Carleton shook Lenny's hand. "You be sweet to Vickie or I might dust off the old Carleton and pay you a visit."

Still grinning, he drove away.

Rosie glanced at the unmade bed. "Room service here isn't tip top. I notice a strand of hair on one of those pillows that doesn't come close to matching yours."

"I had company," Lenny said.

"I heard from the Fremont County medical examiner. He attributed Warner's death to hypothermia. Alcohol was a contributing factor. The sheriff didn't find much of value or interest in Warner's tent—except for nearly a thousand dollars in cash money. A man in Laramie said he paid Warner for two cameras and different lenses. Police there and here are trying to locate a next of kin."

Lenny handed her the inventory of everything removed from the cottage. "What's left?" she asked.

"A few books boxed up to take to the village library. Mr. DeFoe said they're not worth anything. Warner wasn't much of a reader."

Rosie lifted the shade and stared out at the parking lot. "Folks suspect Warner photographed carnal activity, but the photos he kept in his office of birds and a couple of deer are the only ones we know about. DeFoe might not have searched carefully enough."

The fifth try the Jeep sputtered awake. The stores on College Street were beginning to open. "Not counting students, what's the village population?"

"About three thousand," Lenny said.

He stopped on Forest Road and pointed where Carleton was going to build houses. Rosie asked if anyone would object. Lenny said he didn't keep up with village politics. He drove past the footing for the new security gate and continued along the west side of the lake past the swimming beach and the dam. The cottage was empty. The windows had been cleaned and sunlight filled the main room.

Rosie watched Lenny rummage through the books in the box by the door. Almanacs, a guide to medicinal plants, a history of football, an atlas of state maps.

"Much as I travel, I could use the maps," she said.

He handed her the book. A photograph fell out. "I suspect what the girl is smoking isn't tobacco. What do you think?"

"She must be cold with no clothes on."

Rosie settled down next to Lenny and shook out four more photos. "Recognize anyone?"

"A kid I saw New Year's Eve. He had clothes on." Lenny picked up another picture, a Black girl and a white girl pressed against each other. "I've passed the white girl jogging but I've never seen the other one."

"He's up for it." Rosie showed Lenny the print of a naked

girl with a bandanna around her neck watching a boy stepping out of his Jockeys.

"Don't know them either," Lenny said.

"I do." Wade Defoe stood over Lenny's shoulder. "The Black girl is the daughter of a faculty member in sociology. The young man undressing is Bob Herbert's son. Bob lives off a trust fund and travels. The girl watching is Ken Stubbs's daughter. She's a high school senior, same as the Herbert kid."

Rosie asked if Warner had a darkroom.

"He belonged to a photography club," DeFoe said. "They use the college's photo lab."

Rosie guessed there were more photographs somewhere. DeFoe remembered that early in December Warner burned a pile of rubbish and prunings. He could have destroyed the pictures he didn't want anyone to find. He kept the atlas in his office. He probably forgot he had tucked some prints between the pages.

"I'll be outside," Rosie said.

DeFoe discussed refilling the lake and finishing the security gate. The association would buy a new bed for the cottage and a couple of chairs. "If you need anything else, let me know." He wished Lenny good luck and left to meet a client.

Rosie was waiting in the Jeep. "Those photos—I doubt Warner forgot about them." she said.

Lenny drove up the hill to the village and parked in front of Garrick's Photo on Pleasant Street.

Short and stocky, Gene Garrick wore khaki trousers and a blue cardigan. He scuffed his moccasins when he walked. "Let's talk outside," he said. He leaned against the warm bricks of the storefront and lit a cigarette.

Rosie showed him her PI license. "Here's what we have." Gene put on his glasses, and Rosie handed him the pictures. He offered his opinion. The subjects overwhelmed the composition.

"Would you print these?" Rosie asked.

"Depends on the customer."

"Warner. Don't know his first name."

"It's Charley," Gene said. "He wouldn't ask me to print anything. He could do black-and-whites himself at the college. A commercial lab would handle the color work, which is usually what he did. These aren't his."

"Sure?" Lenny asked.

"Warner mostly photographed animals and birds. Dawn was his favorite time. He used long lenses. In these pictures, see how bright it is and how close the photographer is to the subjects." Gene examined the prints again. "The printing's basic drugstore quality. Warner was fussy."

"He might have burned some of his work."

"He was very private. He wouldn't leave something behind that he didn't want anyone to find and comment on or conclude things about the photographer. If he made pictures like those you just showed me, he definitely would have destroyed them."

"You know he died?"

"That's what I mean. He settled his account. Said he might be homeless for a while. He wasn't sure when he'd see me again."

"You know how he died?"

"Froze, the paper said." Gene handed the prints to Rosie.

"Do you belong to the photo club?"

"I pay dues, but I hardly ever join the shoots they plan or listen to the speakers they invite. I don't need to use the college's facilities. I have my own. Most of the members do. A basic darkroom doesn't take up much space. Except for a decent enlarger, most of the equipment isn't expensive."

Lenny drove Rosie back to the motel where she'd left her car. "You don't need to lose any more weight," she said.

IV

Lenny peered over the dam. "Not going to jump, are you?"

"Watching the lake fill up." Lenny looked past Zephyr toward the parking area but didn't see a car.

"I walked," Zephyr said. "Beautiful morning, the world blooming again—lovely. And it's spring break, the students cavorting themselves in various Sodoms by the sea. I was hoping to find you. I want to apologize, at least set the record straight. The committee agreed you were being set up. The point wasn't to take Wallace Wallace down as much as to delve into the matter of tutoring athletes in general and to gauge if there was corruption, how far up it went. What's the expression—the fish rots from the head?"

"Bullard?"

"Indeed." Zephyr pointed across the lake. "Alums like DeFoe encourage the college to excel in sports to increase alumni giving. We don't fault that, but it does involve questionable decisions. Bullard has several building projects in mind that require funding. If the money becomes available and the facilities are built, the rap the rating services lay against us, that our science labs and dorms are outdated, will go away.

"If Bullard can recreate the campus and upgrade the faculty by increasing salaries, he will burnish his own reputation and perhaps end up president at an Ivy or one of the little Ivies he's always going on about.

"As for Bliss, he aspires to coach in Division I, and he might get a chance if his program makes a significant turnaround. How he must miss Wallace Wallace."

"Sounds as if Fleck is the only winner."

"The trustees canceled his professorial honor. However, one of our alums elected to the legislature in Raleigh collected enough money to pay off Fleck's mortgage. So often what appears as a generous gesture is, in fact, a pay-off. You can guess the reason."

"Fleck provided the evidence against me."

"That was the agreement. However, Lenny, we believe there is a piece of missing evidence that Fleck could not provide." Zephyr put his hand on Lenny's shoulder. "At Quigley's meeting, you alluded to it, a book report that Wallace didn't write and probably couldn't have written attached to a page with Wallace's name typed on it, which caused you to write the report you did and switch them. You may not like Quigley but respect him for his ability to sniff out academic maleficence no matter how well concealed. He thinks four people saw the report—the person who wrote it, Fleck, Bullard, and you. He guesses Bullard made the document disappear."

Zephyr shaded his eyes and watched a pair of ducks circling each other in the water. "Anything you want to add our speculations?" Lenny shook his head.

"We're all sorry about Warner, but we're glad you're on board. I realize this isn't what you planned, Lenny, but give it time. You're destined for better things."

They walked to the parking area together. "Miss M never runs out of projects. If you're short of cash, she could provide an opportunity to earn a bit."

"Does she photograph anymore?"

"She used to be very serious about it, real work, not snapshots like I showed you. I was envious. One year we each had exhibitions. Her work was praised. Mine was panned. I made no secret of my disappointment. I blame myself for her cutting back, treating photography more as a casual hobby than art."

"If she's home, I might stop by and show her some prints we found in the cottage."

"Some of Warner's birds preening and pecking?"

"Activity of the human variety. You want a ride?"

"No, I need the exercise."

"Cream or sugar?" Miss M asked.

"Black," Lenny said. She filled their mugs, and he followed her outside. They sat at the picnic table by the lake. He handed her the photographs.

"Oh, my. These were in a book in Warner's cottage?"

"I think I was meant to find them."

"They aren't Warner's work." Miss M patted her apron. "I forgot my smokes. Would you be a dear? They're on the counter by my purse. My lighter too."

Dandelions dotted the grass. Lenny remembered picking them for a bouquet. His mother had rubbed his cheeks until the yellow came off on him. Then she lipsticked his mouth and shadowed circles around his eyes. Going to send you to clown school, she said. It was unusual to see her happy.

Lenny read the address on the envelope sticking out of Miss M's handbag: "M Murray, PO Box 53, Prester, NC." The envelope was postmarked Prester. He felt as though Miss M had left it for him to see.

> *Dear M,*
>
> *Remember the book you recommended,* The Spy Who Came in from the Cold? *I never did get around to reading it. I never saw the movie either. But I think of myself as a spy of sorts living the way I do. I certainly inhabit night and the edges of things, and I am rather good at it. I don't mean to spy on people, but without intending to I have observed various transactions, some slightly criminal, the young receiving envelopes—drugs I assume—in exchange for cash, and some involving the heart or lower body parts, exchanges of gratification consummated sometimes in a car but most often in hillside rendezvous. One Bower resident has a regular schedule of different men. I can tell you what day it is by which man it is. Of course, I have also witnessed much bad behavior and overheard many unpleasant arguments.*
>
> *Yes, it is time for me to come out of the cold, or my version of it, yet I find myself reluctant to do so. My body has returned to the physical place I left. In my mind I am where I was the weeks I prepared myself years ago to leave. I have resolved many of my conflicts and*

confusions and put away much of my anger. However, I am not completely ready to give up the shadows. Soon, though, I promise I will.

Often, in one of my disguises, I have passed close to you, most recently at the market where I shoplifted a jar of Skippy, which is often my main source of nutrition. My breath must be disgusting. I hope not to offend you when I cast off my disguises and encounter you face to face.

Be patient. I am very good at what I do, and now the weather is warm again and the hillsides are sweet with shade, I am content to linger. A pleasure, too, to spy upon the young man I have heard called Lenny. The other evening I approached the cottage where he lives, where once the venial Mr. Warner lived, and stood a long while watching him shower himself the way he used to behind his trailer.

I feel I have fallen in love with him. And I sense he senses me watching, waiting, wanting.

Miss M tipped a cigarette out of the pack and tapped it on the table. "Have you showed the photos to anyone else?"

"Mr. Garrick. He agrees with you. Not Warner's work."

"Donna McGoon's, I'd say. She's got a basic SLR Pentax and a couple of different lenses and photographs constantly. Her friends aren't always happy with her doing it. This young man removing his underwear, for example—a decisive moment he might regret. I taught her some basic darkroom procedures and let her use my equipment until she got some of her own. Who knows—she missed Woodstock, but she might put together a collection documenting the rituals and transgressions of local teens."

Miss M pushed her cigarette into the pack. "I'm trying to quit. More coffee?"

"Need to patrol," Lenny said.

They walked back to the kitchen. Lenny set his empty mug in the sink. He glanced at the opened handbag and envelope and wondered how many letters Haley had written to Miss M.

May turned steamy. Lenny took down the winter signs at the swimming beach and put up the summer signs warning against unaccompanied bathing and loud music, as well as the requirement that residents and guests refrain from alcohol use, wear appropriate clothing, and deposit trash and unwanted articles in the barrels provided by the Residents' Association.

By the middle of June, sons and daughters home for the summer—the college crowd—occupied the beach, sunning and drinking and leaving their bottles and cans for Lenny to collect and dispose of when he patrolled after attending his summer school class.

In July most of the college crowd had jobs, and older residents smeared themselves with sunscreen and took over the beach until late afternoon. Evenings were humid and buggy, and the beach was mostly deserted. However, Mr. Dye reported the frequent presence of marijuana smoke in the air close to a thicket of willows at the far end of the beach. Lenny reminded him that the association had asserted no objection to recreational drug use. To do so would acknowledge an activity the residents preferred to overlook for the benefit of the community at large.

August. Lenny had avoided Red's, but it was time to find out what was on his mind. Red and Cliff were discussing someone named Tom Schiff.

"When Mayor Weaver was in here yesterday, he said he had heard a rumor that Schiff was planning to run against him. I told him not to sweat it."

"Prester must be the only municipality in the state to hold an election in August—dog days, for God's sake. It should be illegal."

"I think it is, but for a hundred years no one has objected," Red commented.

"Hardly anyone votes. What was it? Out of seventeen hundred registered, about eight hundred cast a ballot?"

"August was chosen because most faculty are away. Even back then they were considered too liberal or too something to vote the way folks who actually worked for a living thought people should vote."

"Shiftless Schiff—what's his profession?" Cliff asked.

"Orthodontist. Wires and pliers."

"I guess that counts as work."

"Only sees patients three afternoons a week. Plenty of extra time to run the village."

Red asked Lenny if he intended to vote. "Hadn't thought about it," he answered.

Red turned to Cliff. "There you go. The young don't take their civic responsibilities seriously."

"Go easy on him, Red. There's more monkey business in politics than there is in basketball."

Lenny left them laughing about Mono Mono and walked down the street to the hardware store and gave Buck a key to duplicate. Smith came in and Buck asked him if the village had rules about the size and locations of election signs. Smith said signs weren't usually a problem, but this year the opposition had planted them everywhere. Weaver might have a fight on his hands. Buck reminded them that Schiff was Black. The village wasn't going to elect a Black mayor.

The Jeep expressed its opposition to hot and humid, but it got Lenny back to the cottage. He dined on a Swanson dinner, napped, then began to type an essay for the independent study course that would give him enough credits to graduate.

The security gate was installed. Lia didn't bother to knock. Someone—"Wasn't me," she said—had put the gate out of working order. She lifted a bottle from her tote. "Old vine grenache, highly recommended." She looked around the room. "Drink it here or at the beach? Warm enough for swimming."

"New Residents' Association rule—no alcohol at the beach and no music after nine."

"Rules are made to be broken."

"Plenty of residents share that opinion."

Lia pointed to the book on Lenny's table. "*All the King's Men*—what's it about?"

"Politics. Corruption."

"You have one, you have the other."

"You sound like Mr. Barrow."

"Not sure what Maisie saw in him except a bank account she could borrow from. *Barrow* from, you could say. No doubt Cliff accepted her body as collateral." She shrugged. "Maisie's choice. It wouldn't have been mine."

"Where *is* she this summer?"

"Hammering and painting sets and understudying a couple of parts at a summer theater on Cape Cod."

Lia set the bottle on the desk. "What about that Black girl you had feelings for?"

"She moved to Raleigh."

While Lia explored the kitchen for a corkscrew and glasses, Lenny found the bracelet. "Let's go to the beach," he said.

She nestled the glasses into her tote. Lenny carried the wine. They stopped in the parking area and took a blanket out of her car and continued down the hill toward the water. "Moon's as bright as a reading light."

"You make that up?" Lenny asked.

"A Jerry Jeff Walker song. Favorite of Maisie's. Can't recall the rest."

Lia spread the blanket. Lenny opened the wine and filled the glasses. She said, "Talking about politics and corruption, I noticed one of Mayor Weaver's minions stuck a campaign poster on that gate thing you think is going to keep people out."

"Is Weaver corrupt?"

"Of course. The village isn't the peaceable kingdom people want to believe it is. You don't get a contract to do anything in town or even in the county unless Weaver gets his cut. I mean, he owns a paving company, and our roads receive constant attention. He does business as far away as Charlotte."

"What's he need the mayor's job for?"

"Cover. Besides, no one else has wanted it, until now."

The wine was good. Lenny poured himself more. Lia finished hers, kicked off her sandals, and ambled toward the shore. At the water's edge she lifted her T-shirt over her head and pushed down her jeans. She wasn't wearing anything else. She swished the water with her foot, turned around, and picked up her clothes.

She stood over Lenny. "Too cold?" he asked.

"Not in the mood to get wet. At least not that way," she said.

"I have something you lost." He reached up and handed her the bracelet. "L M T, Lia Margaret Thorne. It's yours, isn't it?"

She seemed surprised and sad at the same time. "It's Amelia Margaret Thorne—if you want to know."

They heard a click. A dark figure faded into the shadows. "That's that," she said.

Lenny admired the way she walked up the hill as if being naked didn't matter.

⁂

Next morning Schiff examined the piece of the broken arm still bolted in place. "Is this contraption intended to keep visitors out or residents in?"

"It's meant for security," Lenny said.

"You haven't answered my question. Does it protect Bower residents from the rest of us, or the rest of us from certain Bowerites best quarantined from genteel society?"

"Give me some names."

"DeFoe—you don't get as rich as he is without cheating and taking from the poor. Merkle—he defends every scofflaw in the county. The state ought to rescind his law license. Also, a scurrilous accountant, whom I shall not name. And you. I've heard Bower folks joking you should run for mayor, like a compromise candidate. Not Black. Not white. Grey."

"Dr. Schiff, the only running I do is an occasional loop round the lake."

"Do you favor me or Mr. Weaver?"

"I'm not registered to vote."

"Do you have an opinion as to which candidate—Weaver or me—would be the better choice?"

"Probably you?"

"No *probably* about it. I *am* the better candidate. Would you consider hustling up to the village offices and registering to vote?"

"Yes."

"Would you go so far as to adhere one of my campaign stickers to your bumper?"

"My Jeep, but not to the association vehicle I patrol in."

"Excellent. Fair warning, though. A sticker favoring my election will displease many of your neighbors."

"I'll take a chance."

"That's my slogan—Vote Schiff. Take a Chance." He reached into his car and brought out a sticker. "What do you think?"

"Black and white."

"Correct. No reds or blues, no bright colors. Black and white is what the election is about. It's 1981. Look around and listen to what people say and you'd assume it's 1961, or 1861. Things got to change." Schiff studied Lenny's mouth. "You have very straight teeth."

"Is that important?"

"Is to me. I'm an orthodontist. Don't have too many patients. Most Black kids have parents who can't afford what I do, and I only charge enough to get by. Fortunately, there's clients who drive over from Greensboro to allow me to indulge in a decent bottle of rye from time to time, but don't tell anybody. Otherwise, the all-powerful Weaver will print cartoons of me, feet up on my desk, smoking a cigar, and sipping whiskey to make me out as the stereotype of the Negro politician the white community expects me to be." Schiff loosened his tie. "Now, I was fixin' to leave some campaign material on residents' doorsteps. May I proceed?"

"Of course, but don't expect a warm welcome."

"I never do. I keep up with college activities, the search for a new president and all that. Let me inquire—have you recent knowledge of Wallace Wallace?"

"He returned to Georgia. He was collecting eggs in the family's chicken coop. A rattlesnake was keeping warm under one of the hens and bit him. The venom and a tetanus infection affected the nerves in his shooting hand. Eventually he'll recover."

"I'm sorry I asked."

"I'm sorry for Wallace."

⁂

To register to vote required two visits to the town clerk. He wanted evidence Lenny was eligible to be a state resident—college students usually weren't. He had to affirm he didn't receive financial help from his mother and to the best of his knowledge she didn't include him as a dependent on her taxes. He had to list all the places he'd lived in the state and for how long. He had to produce 1099s or W2s from employers. The clerk checked his driver's license and wanted him to explain what state taxes he had paid, when, and how much.

"The clerk told me it was the last day to file to run for office."

"Were you tempted?" Rosie asked.

"I already have a job."

"And a diploma."

Lou was listening. She produced a special bottle of tempranillo, compliments of the house. Lenny shook his head. Rosie asked if he had something better in mind.

"A stakeout," he said.

"Never liked those," Rosie said. "Too much coffee and no place to pee."

Zephyr was away on his annual Atlanta visit. Lenny had found a comfortable patch of grass concealed by willows where he could sit and watch the Harrisons' house and the lake. The first two nights Miss M was alone she had turned off the lights and gone to bed before ten o'clock. Tonight the kitchen lights stayed on.

Eleven o'clock. Owls called back and forth, the cricket choir joining in. The backdoor opened. A person stood in the light long enough for Lenny to see a woman carrying something rolled up under her arm. She walked across the lawn toward the lake and disappeared behind the shed where Zephyr stored tools and a mower. A few minutes later a canoe and a kneeling figure appeared paddling toward the middle of the lake. The boat drifted while the paddler raised up, holding onto the gunwales until balanced enough to lift what she had carried under her arm, spread it on the water, and pour something over it. A small flame flared, spread, and dimmed.

Lenny walked along the shoreline. When the canoe nudged the slope of sand past the shed, he reached for the bow and steadied the boat while the paddler stepped out. He handed her a package of crackers. “Mr. Grey, are you here to nab me?” she asked.

Miss M came out of the house. “Zeph will be relieved the painting is gone.” She put her arm around Haley, who promised to meet Lenny the next day, Warner’s cottage. A couple of things Lenny needed to know. Then she leaned her head on Miss M’s shoulder. They crossed the lawn and disappeared into the house.

The next afternoon Lenny checked the cars parked at the swimming beach for Bower stickers. Nine people splayed themselves on towels in the sun, two splashed each other in the water. He wrote down the plate number of a yellow Mustang without a sticker. A camera bag was on the front seat.

“Mine,” Donna McGoon said. Her bathing suit was small and white and nearly transparent. Her tanned skin glistened with iodine and baby oil.

Lenny tapped his notebook. “Stop by the office for a sticker.”

“I have something to show you.” She edged by him. “No, it’s not my tits. Don’t get your hopes up. Or anything else.”

She took a folder from the glove box. “Photographs,” she said. She found the one she wanted and handed it to him. “The night I shot this I didn’t expect to see a truck. Ordinarily I wouldn’t have wasted film on it, but it shouldn’t have been where it was, the overgrown road to that old farm near where your trailer used to be. The driver sprayed something out of the back of the truck. Whatever it was, it didn't smell bad, but I don't think it's healthy. The driver didn't appear to be the friendly type, so I didn't ask any questions."

"Did he see you?"

"No. And the truck made too much noise for him to hear anything, like you did when Maisie's mother was in the nude for love and you weren't, and you heard my shutter click and called it a night. I'm saving for a Leica that's so silent it wouldn't scare a sparrow."

"Why were you there in the first place?"

"Call it my modus operandi, wandering in the dark. A couple of times when you worked nights for Warner, you almost spotted me. Sorry I ruined your evening with Mrs. Thorne."

"You didn't." Lenny scanned the Mustang. "Nice car."

"A birthday present—eighteen next week. I want to have a party, but Uncle Wade said I could only invite people who live here. Most of my friends live in the village. He said to ask you."

"How many?"

"A dozen. I realize I've been a pain in the ass. Maybe we could take our relationship in a new direction. Two weeks from now I leave for college. I don't spend all my nights taking pictures."

"What do you think is going on in this one?"

"Something illegal."

"What's your uncle think?"

"He thinks I have enough photographs for an interesting book. Trouble is, I could make more money from people paying me not to publish the pictures they're in than selling a few copies to weirdos interested in a photo collection of my spoiled friends."

"Is Maisie included?"

"You bet—a party last Christmas, a drink in hand, clothing askew. One of her mom, too. Poolside, stars and moon. Enough light I didn't need a long exposure. The other night, you and her, even with fast film, wide aperture, and a bit of help from the moon, there wasn't enough detail in the negative to print. I have a nice shot of you under your solar shower, though. Copies are always available."

"Not sure I can afford your prices."

"Alternate arrangements are encouraged. Ten friends?"

"What college are you going to?"

"Blackmail State—is that your guess?"

"Seriously."

"Dartmouth. Uncle Wade checked you out. You turned down a scholarship there."

"Ten guests," Lenny said. "You're responsible."

❧

Five o'clock. Mr. Dye took over. Lenny showered, put on his cleanest shirt and jeans, and poured himself an oaky California white. He smelled the rain before he heard it on the roof.

Haley arrived before the first clap of thunder. She had acquired her tie-dyed T-shirt from the Vintage Shop and her white skirt from a clothesline in the village. A habit, she agreed, she needed to break.

Lenny gave her a towel to dry her hair. He filled a glass for her. Rain fell harder. Lightning flashed. The refrigerator ceased humming. "Why?" he asked and left it up to her where to begin.

"I need to finish what I started," she said. "To come full circle."

"How many people know you're back?"

"Miss M, of course. You. I wrote Avis, but I haven't seen him yet."

"Avis?"

"The house with lots of glass across the lake. My therapist. Henry Avis. Rent-a-shrink."

"Miss M knew where you were?"

"I promised to write her. Over the years I mailed the letters to a PO box she rented under her maiden name." Haley laughed. "Maiden name sounds very Victorian now."

"Carleton Pyle told me Warner assaulted you."

"Carleton was a handful. Maiden's sweet dream when it came to sex."

"What about Warner?"

"It was what Carleton said, only rape is the word I used when I wrote what happened and left the note in my boots for Carleton to find. Warner knew where I was camping. He thought he'd give me a going-away present—him and Pudge Weaver. Pudge only watched."

"The mayor?"

"Wasn't then."

"So you *did* thumb a ride and made it to Mexico."

"A few bumps and bruises along the way, but mostly safe and sound." Haley laughed again. "A long way it was."

"Zephyr Harrison—you burned the portrait he painted."

"He loved me more than I loved myself. Maybe still does—the me that went away."

"What about Miss M?"

"She loves me too."

"The daughter she never had?"

"It's more complicated than that."

"Carleton only found the boot with the note."

They finished their wine. The rain was letting up. The refrigerator hummed again. The sky brightened. Lenny refilled their glasses. Haley asked what he was thinking.

"That after you left, Weaver found both boots before Carleton did, took one, and left the one with your note accusing Warner."

"Possible. They acted like friends, but they weren't. I remember Pudge egging Warner on, insulting his manhood if he allowed a spoiled brat like me who protested against war and snubbed men like him who had fought against the Commies and for the American way. I doubt Pudge has ever fought for anything but himself."

"Write a letter to the *View*, tell what happened. The village might elect a new mayor."

"I avoid politics in any form. Besides, I'm not sure how many people would believe me. I was taught to forget the bad things that happen. A new day was on the horizon."

"What's yours going to look like?"

"I'm going to become Miss Normal—buy new clothes, eat nutritious meals, find a proper place to live, own a car. I kept a set of keys to the MG I sold. I don't regret taking a drive."

"A secretarial job with the college would allow you to enroll in a course each semester."

"I don't want to be a student again."

"Have you met Rosie?"

"I've heard of her and why she's here."

"What about your father?"

"One step at a time. I'll meet with Rosie and let her break the news. It's what Daddy is paying her for."

"What are you doing for money?"

"I'm still entitled to what my mother left me. I may need a lawyer."

"And time. What about now?"

"I'll find something."

"A bed?"

"Miss M's guest room while Zeph's away."

"Then?" Haley pointed to Lenny's couch.

LENNY FOUND A STICKER for Donna's car and added its plate number to the list of residents' vehicles. Henry Avis's Plymouth was the first one: Vanity plate L M T L M T.

Mr. Avis ("*Doctor*, but call me Henry") let Lenny into his office by the side door near the kitchen. Henry's jeans were pale from wear and washing. His sneakers were coming apart. Lenny remembered seeing him before, at Oliver's, concentrating on Lia, and later his visit to the pool. His T-shirt read "I Survived Dora."

"Hurricane?" Lenny asked.

"Former spouse." Henry pointed to a chair by a window. He bent his trim body into the chair behind a desk stacked with books and journals. "I'm a voyeur—peoples' minds, peoples' bodies. I know who you are. What's going on?"

"Last night I met Haley Flagg."

"Despite her thrift-shop disguise, I thought I saw her by the dumpster behind the market. She didn't use to limp."

"A disagreement with a lover named Marco. He pushed her off a balcony. She'll tell you all about it."

"I don't have clients anymore. The state revoked my license—no thanks to Lia Thorne." Henry stared out the window, then back at Lenny. "I left a note in her car warning her she wouldn't get away with it, but she did. In retrospect she was less interested in my nursing her mind than satisfying her body. When I ended the relationship, she sent an ethics complaint to the state medical board that I had seduced her. She pointed out that I had been the therapist of a young woman who had gone missing, implying that my proclivity to be sexually interested in my clients might have caused her harm." Henry sighed. "As Vonnegut observed, so it goes."

Lenny pointed to the stack of pages next to Henry's typewriter. "A project," he said, "long in the doing."

"Haley said she needed to finish what she started."

"Haley was nineteen, unhappy, angry, confused, et cetera—about to go off the rails. I encouraged her to do it." Henry held up his hand. "Go where you want to go, do what you want to, need to do, act out of passion—eventually, though, you will stop and take a deep breath and, like it or not, you will go back where you left off—mentally or physically or both—but as a different person, a wiser person, guided by your new-found insights, decorated with your scars. You will retrace your steps, get on track. From where you left off, you will begin again. That's the essence of my therapy. It's what life is—the long and winding road, stepping off, getting on again, making one's way." Henry looked at his fraying sneakers and shook his head. "In case you're wondering, there was no sexual relationship between Haley and me."

"Tell me about your license plate."

"Are *you* the therapist now?"

"Just curious. Someone left me a bracelet with the same letters."

"Love me tender, love me true. Haley's bracelet. We were both Elvis fans."

Lenny stood up to leave.

"Lenny, this election," Henry said, "I've heard a rumor some residents are going to write in your name—the gray candidate."

"A joke that's gotten out of hand."

"So?"

"If Vonnegut wrote something profound about rumors, I've forgotten it."

HALEY WORE A SILK BLOUSE, slacks, and sandals. "Miss M took me shopping." A cookbook lay open on the counter. "Never seen such a clean stove. Ever use it?" Lenny shook his head.

"Zeph returned early. Mixed emotions followed." Haley took a package wrapped in butcher paper out of the refrigerator. "You're not a vegetarian, are you?" Lenny shook his head again.

They ate spicy chicken and rice, a recipe Marco had taught her. Hate the man, love his cooking. One day he couldn't get enough of her, the next he wanted her gone.

The pinot gris was too sweet, but it was what Lenny had.

Haley weighed a hundred pounds, her body more a gymnast's than a horsewoman's. Marco didn't think she would land so hard, that she could float like a leaf.

They washed the dishes and opened a second bottle. Haley talked, Lenny listened. Fall her freshman year Zephyr had a show at the college gallery. She admired one of his paintings and commissioned him to paint her portrait the way she wanted it—an image of her that would puzzle and anger her father, never a faithful husband and now married to a woman once encouraging as a riding coach but changed into a selfish stepmother. Zephyr fell in love with Haley. At first Miss M took the place of the mother Haley missed, but...there were looks and touches and whispered secrets, a sweet melancholy they shared as they abided by social rules and expectations. Haley tuned into the counterculture and dropped out. Henry Avis encouraged her. Rage, rage—you will be the better for it.

Haley borrowed one of Lenny's shirts to sleep in. After midnight the thunder woke him. Haley called out his name. Wrapped in a sheet, she huddled on the couch. In the silence he sensed what was there and never was before. Don't expect love, take what you can get. But his mother had it wrong.

"Stay with me," Haley said.

❧

RED SQUINTED AT LENNY. "You vote?"

"Of course he did," Cliff said. "See the black ink on his hand?"

Red mixed Lenny's Coke. "You don't care for beer?"

"He's a wine snob," Cliff said. "Look at his upturned nose."

Red eyed Lenny again. "Cliff's out of sorts today. His doctor told him to lose weight."

"What's he know?" Cliff mumbled.

Red asked what Cliff knew about the election. "Quite a turnout. The clerk estimates about twelve hundred voted. From the ballots he's seen, it's going to be close."

Red opened another beer and handed the can to Cliff. "Any write-ins?"

"He said he saw a bunch."

"Weaver used to be more helpful to people, or at least he pretended to be. Lately he's been mean and taken his position for granted. If he loses, it's because too many folks who always voted for him stayed home this time."

"They should have considered staying home was like voting for Schiff."

"I still believe Weaver will pull through. What's up with the Pyle project?"

"Done for is the rumor. Weaver will announce tomorrow why he and the planning committee are going to deny final permitting for construction and septic. Public invited. Comments welcome. I can't imagine more than a handful of citizens showing up."

"Not sure, Cliff. The village is turning testy. Schiff's to blame. Too much talk of change, like someone throws a switch and presto, things happen. Change has got to be gradual."

"You're right. The folks moving here don't understand that. You agree, Mr. Grey?"

Red squinted at Lenny again—a warning. Be careful how you answer. Lenny said he always valued Cliff's opinion.

A room in the basement of the municipal building—one of its yellowing walls decorated with a mural of a flushed and florid Caedmon Prester holding out his arms to strangers, the wooded wilderness behind him.

A lectern for the mayor and a table with chairs for him at the head and five others facing the audience for the members of the village council. Two dozen folding chairs had been set out, plenty for the number of townspeople expected to attend the meeting. Several minutes before Weaver was scheduled to call it to order, the town clerk gave him a second piece of bad news. More chairs were needed.

By three o'clock Lenny counted thirty-one in attendance. Though the mayor held a gavel, the audience quieted as soon as he approached the lectern. The room was small. No microphone required.

"Welcome," he said. He took a slip of paper out of his jacket pocket. "The clerk has tallied the results of the recent election. One thousand one hundred and four votes were cast—503 for me, 402 for Schiff, and 199 write-in ballots for..." Weaver hesitated. "I see Schiff but I don't see—"

"Here," Lenny said.

"One hundred ninety-nine votes for that man."

The audience mumbled and Weaver gaveled for silence. "Those of you familiar with our rules recall that the winner must obtain a majority of all the votes cast. Such is not the case. The rules further stipulate if no candidate receives fifty percent of the votes, a new election shall be called within twenty days. Its winner will be the candidate who receives the most votes no matter the number cast. In order to compete, Mr. Grey, you must formally file to have your name on the ballot and pay the appropriate fee."

Weaver pointed to a man who raised his hand. "Does that mean no write-ins?"

"More or less."

"Where does it say that?"

"I just said it."

"Yes, but in the village rules or whatever we go by, is it written no write-ins the second time around?"

"Any person can write in his name or another the second time around. However, the town attorney has determined since a hundred and ninety-nine people voted for Mr. Grey, he has become officially involved in the process and he is no longer a possible write-in, by which we usually mean an unofficial candidate, and therefore must register as a candidate and put up some money. After all, since we need to print new ballots, Mr. Grey should pay his fair share."

Another man stood up and fanned his face with his straw hat. "What difference will it make? If the same pattern holds, the next time *you* win and Grey, write-in or not, finishes third."

"Yes," said Weaver. "I would win. Can we get on with it, this meeting, which is about what is referred to as the Pyle project since it involves land in the family of Black farmers named Pyle?" Weaver held up a sheaf of papers. "I have here deeds and tax records if anyone cares to trace the property's legal history."

Silence. "Good." Weaver reached into his jacket, took out a single sheet of paper, and unfolded it. "What is not in the legal documentation is this—the recent result of soil tests conducted on the property to determine its fitness and suitability for a major housing development. The bottom line—it failed. The land is contaminated with PCBs, polychlorinated biphenyls. They are as new to me as to you, but I can tell you they are extremely toxic. They are dangerous. We cannot allow building of any sort. Based on the findings of the planning committee, I and the council are in unanimous agreement to deny permits for any and all proposed construction or public use."

A woman raised her hand. "Where are these CBPs from?"

"PCBs, ma'am. They do not naturally occur in nature. They result from the manufacturing process of certain devices and were put there. Illegally, of course."

"What devices?" a man asked.

"Electric equipment. Transformers, for example."

"They don't build those here."

"I'm aware of that, sir."

"Are you aware of where they might come from?" the man with the straw hat asked.

"Could be Durham or Raleigh or even Winston-Salem. Who knows?"

"Or Timbuktu," a woman said. "Are you investigating?"

"We tried. No leads. A dead end," Weaver said.

Schiff stood. "Mayor—"

"Make it brief."

"I got this photograph." He raised it up. "I hold it over my head for all to see, but I'm really holding it over *your* head, Mayor."

"Meaning what, exactly?"

"You have a financial interest in a trucking company, do you not?"

"I have many financial interests."

"Perhaps you could identify this truck as one of yours." He passed the photo forward. "I have several prints, if anyone wants one."

Weaver examined the picture. "Dark night, dark truck, no plate visible, no markings." He shrugged.

"Person who made the photograph said the plate was muddied over, and she couldn't read it."

"Does the person have a name?"

"I don't care to put the photographer in a difficult situation."

"This isn't Mafia country. You make it sound like someone might threaten harm."

"Many here know whose country you believe it to be—"

"Mr. Schiff, this isn't the time or place for one of your campaign riffs on our racial history. This photograph—are you accusing me of something?"

"Denying Mr. Pyle and his associate the opportunity to develop needed residential accommodation."

"Needed by whom? If you're wanting to buy a house, I got a couple to sell located in a delightful project called Evergreen."

"I've seen them—shacks is what they are, and what you call Evergreen isn't green. It's brown and hot and dusty in the summer, brown and cold and muddy in the winter. Some shacks lack running water."

"Depends on how much rain we get and who doesn't pay their utility bill."

"Mayor, we can discuss housing later. I'm suggesting your truck dumped polluting chemicals on Mr. Pyle's property—."

"*Suggesting*, not accusing?"

"And you had knowledge of the illegal activity."

"Sounds like an accusation. You quit straightening teeth and taken up lawyering? You talk like one from an old TV show. Careful you don't get cited for practicing law without a license."

Schiff turned to the audience. "Officer Smith stopped a similar truck and told the driver his license plate was unreadable. The driver emptied a water bottle on a rag and cleaned the plate. He said he must have backed into a dirt pile. Smith told the driver to go on, but he copied down the plate number. The truck is registered to Our Land Transport, which happens to be one of Mr. Weaver's many financial interests."

"Doesn't mean I take part in its daily operation or am aware of what it's transporting," Weaver replied.

"This was a night operation."

Weaver sighed. "Mr. Schiff, I called this meeting to make public why the planning committee denied a permit. It is not the opportunity to debate the origin of the issue on which we based our denial."

"When would the opportunity occur?"

"I'll confer with the council and let you know."

Lenny watched the room empty. Weaver followed him to his car. "Complications, Mr. Grey, always complications. Nothing is ever simple and straightforward."

"Am I a complication?"

"Indeed, you are, Mr. Grey. Indeed, you are. What thoughts do you have about officially throwing your hat into the ring?"

"Haven't decided anything."

"People don't really know much about you other than your dustup with the college about supplying illegal assistance to an athlete. My advice is to save your powder for another time. Make the acquaintance of more of the residents. If I am elected, it will be my last term, and you would have a good opportunity to take my place. Wade DeFoe thinks highly of you and that counts."

"I appreciate your advice, sir." Lenny opened the Jeep's door.

Weaver closed it. "Something else to consider. The road around the lake needs repaving. I bid low. The Residents' Association knows my men will do a good job."

"I'm sure they will." Lenny opened the Jeep's door again.

"Thing is, Mr. Grey, sometimes my hires get a bit boisterous. They'll knock a head or two. Handsome as yours is, we wouldn't want to mess it up."

"No, we wouldn't." Lenny raised himself into the Jeep.

Weaver held onto the door. "The Flagg girl, she living with you?"

"Not exactly."

"Despite her injury, she's a pretty one. I hear Mr. Rudolph hired her to tend his horses and give riding lessons. His stables and what he owns are kind of isolated. Vagrants used to be a problem—them and druggies would camp out on his property. Not unknown for one of them to spook a horse and cause it to throw the rider."

"You've made your point," Lenny said.

Weaver let go of the door. "Good I did. My boys go overboard when they make it for me."

❧

HALEY WAS CHOPPING ONIONS. She wiped her eyes. "People will believe Weaver scared you off."

"I don't want to take away votes from Schiff."

"Can he win?"

"Don't know about the election. Do know that Carleton hired a bulldog of an attorney to go after Weaver for contaminating his land. Rosie is investigating Weaver's activities."

The sky clouded over. They finished supper before the rain began. Lights blinked and went out. The refrigerator lost its hum. They lay together on the couch. Lenny told Haley that Mr. DeFoe had offered to provide the cottage with a generator. "Why spoil things," she said and lifted her skirt and knelt over Lenny. His tongue traced the long scar left by the surgeon who repaired her fractured hip. "Keep going," she said.

The night after the votes were counted and Schiff was the new mayor, neither the Nook nor Oliver's opened. Red hung a funeral wreath on his window. A few cars drove back and forth on College Street, tooting horns.

The cottage had a telephone. Sandy called. The Cat was serving. There was a two-drink limit. Lou told them to seat themselves. Lenny missed the server with impossible tight leggings. Lou said she was now an assistant manager at the motel.

"What about you?" Sandy asked. Lenny told her Cliff Barrow was taking a few weeks off. Mr. Dye needed more hours, and the paper was giving Lenny a chance to report on anything he wanted to and write a column of his own.

They finished their drinks. The village was deserted. Sandy saw it first, the furry shape on the other side of the street, padding down the sidewalk. Haley put her arm around Lenny. They watched until the bear disappeared into the night.

Part III
Starting Over

I

Lenny's Jeep wasn't going to get him to Georgia. The Burlington dealer gave him a deal on a dependable used Cherokee on the condition he mentioned Jeeps in whatever he wrote about his travels. The only column Lenny had written so far was an account of female faculty swarming noon swim and demanding equal use of the pool. Sandy wasn't happy.

Wallace's parents were both tall and wide-shouldered. His mother served up fried chicken, beans, and okra spiced with something local that Lenny wasn't sure he wanted her to identify. They questioned him about the college and Wallace's experience there. He had never told them much about it.

Lewis, Wallace's brother, had found work with the highway department and didn't live at home. Mrs. Wallace held Tanya, Wallace's sister, on her lap. From time to time, she pointed at Lenny and laughed. Wallace's father opened a Lucky Strike tin and showed Lenny the rattles he had cut off the snake that Wallace had written about.

Wallace had moved away as well. Farming peanuts, his father said. He took out a map and showed Lenny where.

Lenny left hill country and drove east. Dusty county roads and long lanes leading to fields, tall trees, barns, and houses with deep porches. Hand-painted signs advertised peaches, pecans, and peanuts. You want Burke's place, a man at the Gulf station said, and gave Lenny directions. Biggest operation around, the man said.

Burke's was easy to find. The name was painted in large letters on a silo that Lenny could see a mile away. A red sun was setting. He turned into the lane. Dogs barked and Mr. Burke himself came down the wide steps of his house, leaning on a cane. Lenny explained that he hoped to find a student he had helped once, how he excelled at basketball, but circumstances had prevented him from staying in school.

Wallace, you mean, Mr. Burke said. He pointed his cane at a building in the distance where his crew bunked. Lenny would find Wallace around the other side. He never came in until it was too dark to see.

Through the windows Lenny saw a television and heard men laughing. Behind the building was a barn. A torn net hung from the goal nailed to weathered siding. Lenny watched Wallace shoot and the ball bounce back to him. He moved left to right, then right to left, dodging imaginary defenders. Twenty-five shots before he missed.

Lenny knew from Wade DeFoe that Wallace had declined to enroll in school in Florida. He knew from Wallace's mother that the young man had read a book most every week, and most every night he filled a page with words. He wrote about neighbors, what they looked like, their characters, what they did for work, and the hope of heaven of which they sang. She'd given Lenny one to read.

Meander was our mule's name. Clea Tyson was the name of the girl I loved. Dark eyes, wide lips, a mouth you wanted to kiss. Her daddy said he would let me marry her if I would give him the mule. Clea's brothers, Newt and Woodrow, both gangly and mouths full of crooked teeth, were against it. Their ma had died, and Clea was a good cook. If she left, they reckoned they would starve. They decided to steal Meander and hide him where I wouldn't find him.

The sheriff long suspected Mr. Tyson stilled whiskey, but no matter how many times he tried, he could not discover where Mr. Tyson produced his product, which was much favored by those neighbors who did not believe celebrating with potent spirits would condemn them in the eyes of the most powerful spirit of all. Although I was on guard, the brothers eluded my caution. When I went to fetch Meander, he was gone.

Meander has a peculiar habit. He likes to rub against things—fence posts, sides of barns, whatever. I discovered traces of his fur on the bark of trees and was able to follow the direction the brothers led him, which ended up being the place where Mr. Tyson made his whiskey. Reluctantly, he agreed to return Meander if I forgot where I had found him.

I could have Clea too.

Light faded. Darkness surrounded them. Wallace said, "Mr. Lenny, I knew you'd find me. Knew it in my bones."

"Ready to start again?" Lenny asked.

"If the school will have me," Wallace said.

"Bliss is gone, but the new coach said to tell you that you are most welcome to rejoin the team." The NCAA would require some paperwork to square things. They were fussy that way, but everything would be put right.

"Everything?" Wallace said.

"As much as possible," Lenny said.

About the Author

Christopher Brookhouse is the author of numerous works of poetry and fiction, among them *Running Out*, which earned the Rosenthal Award from the American Academy of Arts & Letters; *A Selfish Woman*, nominated for the National Book Award; and *Fog, the Jeffrey stories*, winner of the biennial New Hampshire fiction prize.

His most recent works include a 4-book series about aspiring writer-turned-sheriff Gus Salt, set in post WWII North Carolina: *A Pinch of Salt*, *Percy's Field*, *Nolan's Cross*, and *A Mind of Winter*—and *Messing with Men*, a story of old murder and the colliding lives of three retirees on an island in Florida.